Spence at Marlby Manor

Michael Allen

First published in 1984 by Dell Publishing Co. Ltd.

This edition published in 2016 by Endeavour Press Ltd.

One

It began with a barbed bouquet.

Lady Dinnister loved flowers. She was now seventy-two, and arthritis in her hips made it difficult for her to walk, even with a stick, but in her younger days she had spent many happy hours working in the garden of Marlby Manor.

The village of Marlby lay eight miles southwest of Wellbridge, the county town of Southshire; it was a small village of some three hundred inhabitants. Marlby Manor was located to the west of the village proper, on the road to Sixton-on-Weal.

The house was Elizabethan in origin, but two wings had been added in the nineteenth century, together with a seven-foot-high wall surrounding the entire property. The wall was five miles long in all, enclosing extensive grounds with a landscaped lake, a stream, and a wood. In the old days the grounds had been maintained by a small army of gardeners, who had specialised in topiary work, clipping the yew hedges and the boxwood into lions, unicorns, and crowns. More recently, the army of workers had been reduced to one elderly head gardener and two boys, but the lawns were still kept tidy, and the flowerbeds — though much reduced in size — were still a source of joy to the lady of the manor.

On the morning of Monday the twentieth of August, Lady Dinnister was in her sitting room on the first floor of the west wing. The sitting room had been her hideaway for well over forty years, a private place where she could retreat and recharge her batteries in order to go on functioning as a wife and mother. Now, with her husband and daughter both dead, and with her mobility much reduced by arthritis, the sitting room was where she spent most of her days.

But Lady Dinnister was not in any sense a recluse; far from it. The main reason she liked the sitting room so much was that it had windows on three sides, enabling her to look out to the north, the west, and the south; the windows, combined with the height of the first floor and the frequent use of powerful binoculars, enabled her to keep a careful eye on almost everything and everyone in the grounds.

Shortly after 10:45 A.M., Lady Dinnister looked up from her chair at the window and noticed a florist's van turn in through the east gate, coming from the direction of Wellbridge. The van made its way up the half-mile drive, its white roof glinting brightly in the hot summer sun. She watched its approach through her binoculars, only removing them from her eyes when the van arrived at the front door. She turned to the woman who acted as her paid companion and nurse, Miss Fosdyke.

"Well, Emily," said Lady Dinnister, "it looks as if someone is sending us some flowers. Who do you think it could be?"

Miss Fosdyke looked up from the *Daily Telegraph*. She rose to her feet and approached the window. "Goodness knows," she said, peering down at the florist's van through her bifocals. The driver got out, picked up a cardboard box, and advanced with it towards the front door.

"Perhaps you have a gentleman admirer," suggested Lady Dinnister, quite without malice.

Miss Fosdyke, who was sixty and had never been very attractive to men, took no offence. "I doubt it," she said with a sigh. "It's a little late in the day for that. Perhaps I ought to go down and collect these flowers, or whatever they are."

"Certainly not," said Lady Dinnister. "There are plenty of other people downstairs, most of them a great deal younger and fitter than you or me. Let them bring the flowers up."

"Oh. Very well then," Miss Fosdyke said, and returned to her chair and the *Daily Telegraph*.

Lady Dinnister renewed her reading of the *Financial Times*, but she found her attention wandering. She became annoyed with herself. How childish, she thought, to get all excited over a bunch of flowers at my age. But, despite herself, she could not help wondering who they were from.

Lady Dinnister was a slightly built woman. In her youth she had been wiry; now she merely looked thin, and her wrists were particularly scrawny. But, despite her diminutive frame, there was an air of authority about her. She was not in any way a snob; she was approachable, good-humoured, and kind. But she had an indefinable stamp of authority in her features. Her hair had originally been black; now it was streaked with grey, brushed straight back into a bun. Her pale blue eyes were clear and keen-sighted, and she could manage without glasses for all but the closest work. Heavy lines around her eyes and mouth reflected the pain which had visited her in recent years, but her expression was also marked by determination: a determination not to be beaten by the weakness of mere flesh. She sat up straight, still remembering her childhood training, with a cushion in the small of her back.

Lady Dinnister always dressed well, with an infallible eye for what was appropriate, tasteful, and yet fashionable. Today she was wearing a dark red dress with loose-fitting sleeves, a brooch with eight pearls set around a ruby, and a gold watch linked to a gold bracelet that had once belonged to her grandmother.

After what seemed an unnecessarily long delay, the blue-jacketed butler, Alfred Tanner, brought the box of flowers upstairs to the sitting room. He knocked and came in without pausing for permission, bearing the white cardboard box ahead of him.

"Ah, Tanner," said Lady Dinnister. "About time too. What kept you?"

"Urgent call of nature, ma'am," said Tanner, who would use any excuse in an emergency. The truth was that he had decided to finish his coffee in his own good time "before climbing all those bloody stairs just for a bunch of flowers," as he had commented to the housekeeper.

Lady Dinnister sniffed with disapproval. "Hm," she said. "Well, you're here now, anyway. What have you got for us?"

Tanner put the box down on a small table beside Lady Dinnister's chair. "It's a present from your granddaughter, ma'am," he said. "She rang this morning to say they would be coming."

"Oh," said Lady Dinnister briskly. "How nice. Typical of her to order them from a florist when she's got a garden of about three acres of her own. Still, there we are, that's Elizabeth all over; she can't tell a lupin from a lettuce. I told her that myself."

Lady Dinnister untied the ribbon that was loosely bound around the box and opened the lid.

"Oh, look. Baccarat red roses! How beautiful!"

Lady Dinnister reached into the box, grasped the roses by the stems, and started to lift them out. As she did so, she gave a stifled scream and clutched her right hand with her left, dropping the roses back into the box.

Both Miss Fosdyke and the butler hurried to her side.

"Whatever's the matter?" asked Miss Fosdyke, reaching over to examine Lady Dinnister's hand.

"Something stabbed me," said Lady Dinnister. Her face had turned very pale. "Something stuck into my palm — really deep." She opened her hand to reveal a bright red spot of blood welling out of a puncture wound.

"Dear me," said Miss Fosdyke. "So it did. Hold on, I'll get you a plaster."

Miss Fosdyke crossed to a desk and returned promptly with a box of sticking plasters. Using a piece of lint, she wiped away the excess blood and then stuck a large plaster firmly over the source of it. She noticed as she did so that Lady Dinnister's hand was trembling violently.

"This *has* shaken you up, hasn't it?" she remarked sympathetically.

Lady Dinnister nodded. "Yes," she said, "it has. How silly of me — but you're right. It took me so much by surprise." She turned to the butler. "Well, Tanner, have you found out what caused it?"

"Yes, ma'am." Tanner looked up from the florist's box, which he had been investigating cautiously ever since Lady Dinnister had cried out. He lifted the roses carefully out with his left hand and brought them to show the two women. "Here — look — that's what did it." He indicated a piece of rusty green wire that was twisted round the stems of the roses. One end of it stood out sideways, in precisely the position where anyone reaching into the box in a normal way would close her hand on it.

"My word," said Miss Fosdyke. "How very careless of someone."

Lady Dinnister gazed down at the wire for some moments before she spoke. "Yes," she said at last. "It was careless, wasn't it?"

Miss Fosdyke closed the box of plasters with a firm snap. "Well, that's a nasty, dirty piece of wire, and it's gone a good way into your hand. How long is it since you had an antitetanus injection?"

"Tetanus?"

"Yes."

Lady Dinnister thought about it. "Nineteen thirty-four," she said eventually.

"Oh, well, in that case it's high time you had another. I'll ring Dr. Milton and get him to come and give you one." And with that she returned to the desk and picked up the telephone.

"I'll put the roses in water, ma'am," said Tanner, dropping them back into the box and picking up the ribbon.

"Yes, please do," said Lady Dinnister weakly.

"You look rather shocked, ma'am," said Tanner solicitously. "Perhaps a small glass of brandy?"

Lady Dinnister's eyes suddenly brightened. "Brandy at eleven in the morning," she said wonderingly. "Yes, that is a good idea. But not a small one, Tanner — a large one."

*

Miss Fosdyke did not approve of the brandy, but Lady Dinnister drank it anyway. It put her to sleep for an hour, and she had to be woken up when Dr. Milton arrived shortly after twelve o'clock.

Dr. Milton was in his mid-forties: a short, rather stoutly built man with receding black hair and a ruddy brown complexion. Despite the August heat, he was wearing both a tie and a thick brown sports jacket.

"Wakey, wakey, Lady Dinnister," he said cheerfully, putting his black leather bag down on the table beside her chair.

Lady Dinnister opened one eye. "Oh — it's you."

"Yes indeed. I hear you've had an argument with a bunch of roses."

"Yes," said Lady Dinnister sleepily. She held out her hand, and the doctor peeled back the plaster and examined the wound. "But it hardly seems worth your time."

"Not at all," said Dr. Milton. "Not at all. That looks fairly deep to me, and it's just the sort of hole that germs like. It provides an oxygen-free environment, you see, which is just what they need. We nearly lost a patient through lockjaw last year, so you were quite right to ask me to call. Very sensible."

Five minutes later the doctor had administered the necessary injection and was shown out by Miss Fosdyke. Lady Dinnister, wide awake now, turned on the television set and began to watch a cricket match, which was England against New Zealand. She kept the sound turned down, however; there were very few things in life that Lady Dinnister could not tolerate, but most cricket commentators were among them.

Miss Fosdyke returned in due course and sat down at the desk; she began to write a letter to her niece in Morecambe.

Lady Dinnister watched the television until another English wicket had fallen, and then, without taking her eyes off the television screen, she asked a question.

"Why don't you like him, Fozzie?"

"Emily, please."

"All right. Why don't you like him, Emily?"

"Like who?"

"Dr. Milton, of course."

Miss Fosdyke looked up from her letter. "But I do like him."

"No, you don't. It's obvious. Did you cross swords with him in your hospital days?"

Miss Fosdyke scribbled on, head down. "No, never."

"Well, he's certainly done something to offend you. Perhaps it's his choice of after-shave lotion, but whenever he comes in here, you look as if you had smelt something nasty."

"Absolute rubbish," said Miss Fosdyke placidly.

"Well, maybe it is and maybe it isn't." Lady Dinnister sat up and repositioned the cushion in the small of her back. "Now," she said briskly, "where the hell is my lunch?"

Miss Fosdyke stopped scribbling, turned round, and gave Lady Dinnister one of her sternest looks. "I don't think brandy in the morning quite agrees with us, does it?" she said.

Two

Later that day, towards four o'clock, Lady Dinnister called her secretary upstairs to the sitting room to dictate some letters.

The secretary was a Miss Susan Green, twenty-four years old, nearly six feet tall, with a slim figure, light brown hair, brown eyes, and a clear complexion. She was farsighted and wore glasses to take dictation.

Lady Dinnister was catching up on her correspondence to old friends, several of whom lived abroad; the letters were long, rambling, and thoroughly libellous about everyone from the local member of Parliament to the vicar.

The television was tuned to BBC 2, which was still showing the cricket match, and its volume control was still adjusted so that the commentary was almost inaudible. Lady Dinnister sat with her eyes firmly fixed on the set, her feet supported by a small stool. From time to time she interrupted her dictation to sigh at what she regarded as yet more evidence of the steady deterioration of English batting.

Miss Fosdyke sat with her back to the television, reading a biography of Palmerston; it was a book she had always intended to read since its publication ten years earlier, and now that she was retired from her job as a hospital almoner, she had finally found time to begin.

"Now then, where was I?" asked Lady Dinnister. She had been momentarily distracted from her letter to an elderly cousin in India by a dog running onto the pitch in the cricket match.

Susan Green read back the last sentence: "I myself am in pretty good health for my age, apart from the occasional mishap.'" Susan crossed her legs to give the notepad a firmer support.

"Oh, yes. Carrying on from there, then. Don't cross your legs, dear; it upsets Miss Fosdyke."

Susan blushed uncomfortably and put both feet back on the floor. Miss Fosdyke glanced up over her reading glasses and made a disapproving noise, but it was clearly directed at what she regarded as a slight on her character rather than at the crossed legs.

"Ah yes, apart from the occasional mishap," Lady Dinnister continued. "This morning, for instance, I had a present from my granddaughter Elizabeth. You will remember that some three years ago she married a young man called Vernon Hassett, whom I regarded at the time as a complete and utter twit. Time has confirmed my judgement. However, that is not the point. The point is that Elizabeth has always been a remarkably extravagant young lady with an infallible eye for everything that is both expensive and meretricious. She seems to take the view that if a present does not cost the earth, then it is quite without value. Nevertheless, she is a kindly girl at heart, and today she sent me a present that I am sure — well, fairly sure — was sent without any wish to butter me up. Today, I think I began by saying, is the twentieth of August, which is a little early for Christmas, and my birthday is not till March. Anyway, she sent me a present, which on second thought I am quite convinced has some ulterior purpose, though I suppose it is ungracious of me to say so."

"Very," said Miss Fosdyke without looking up. "Don't you think you'd better tone that down a bit?"

Susan Green looked embarrassed and examined the end of her pencil.

"Certainly not," said Lady Dinnister. "And, anyway, this is a private letter, so m.y.o.b. Now — where was I?"

"Um — 'ungracious of me to say so,'" said Susan in a husky voice. She could never quite get used to this two-way banter between the older women and would certainly never have dared to suggest that Lady Dinnister should tone down anything. On the rare occasions when she had deliberately left out a particularly damning adjective in the typed version of a letter, Lady Dinnister had always inked it back in before signing her name. "I know what I mean," Lady Dinnister had said, "and I don't want any bowdlerising, thank you very much indeed."

"Ungracious of me to say so," Lady Dinnister repeated, going on with her dictation. "Yes, anyway, to cut a very long story short, the gift took the form of a box of roses, which I was pleased to receive, despite the fact that my own garden is more than amply stocked with flowers of every conceivable variety, lovingly tended by my faithful head gardener, Mr. Me Winter. However, the point is that when I reached into the box to take out the roses, my hand was pierced by a piece of dirty wire. I was in such a hurry to lift the roses out that I closed my hand very firmly on the tissue paper, and the wire seemed to go right into my hand in a most peculiarly painful manner. As a result of this trivial incident, I was really quite severely shaken. My dear friend Miss Fosdyke — "

Lady Dinnister gave a sideways glance at her companion, who ignored her.

"My dear friend Miss Fosdyke, with her extensive knowledge of matters medical, advised calling the doctor in order to avoid a nasty attack of lockjaw, so one way and another there was quite a fuss. All because of something that in my younger, fitter days I would have regarded as a mere scratch to be forgotten in a moment or two. It is gradually dawning upon me, though I am greatly reluctant to admit it, that I may be on the verge of beginning to grow old."

Lady Dinnister paused as one of the tail-end English batsmen hit out at a ball pitched on his middle stump. Then, satisfied that the result would be four runs, she continued.

"Lunch made up for the pain and distress quite pleasingly. Old Mrs. Hubbott down the road sold us a chicken — a real chicken, not one of those ghastly frozen things that taste like sawdust. This one had been breathing good, clean country air until the moment the axe caught up with it. Mr. Tanner, the butler, plucked it and drew it, and Hazel, my housekeeper, cooked it most beautifully. Mr. Tanner added one of his famous secret sauces. I was greatly tempted to have a third helping, but Miss Fosdyke advised me that it would not be very ladylike to do so."

"You made a dreadful pig of yourself as it was," said Miss Fosdyke. turning a page of her book.

"Anyway, Florence," dictated Lady Dinnister, "it is now nearly five o'clock and high time I stopped talking, particularly as my secretary is champing at the bit to go off for a walk with my grandson."

Susan looked up. startled. "Oh. Lady Dinnister," she said. "I never so much as mentioned it."

Lady Dinnister smiled. "You didn't need to. my dear. I heard his motorbike come popping up the drive a few minutes ago, just as you did, and I saw the look on your face."

Susan blushed again, a blush that was made all the more intense by the anger she felt for allowing herself to go pink in the first place. There was nothing to be ashamed of in being in love; why on earth did she have to act as if there were?

Lady Dinnister laughed, but kindly. She reached out with her left hand and patted Susan's knee. "Never mind, my dear. I only tease you because I'm jealous. Believe me, I would be only too pleased to be your age if I could. Now, just a couple more sentences. Paragraph. So I will end now, Florence. I hope to hear from you soon that all is well with you and George, and in the meantime I send you my fondest love. There."

Susan drew a line across her pad, mainly to stop herself from standing up immediately. It would be most undignified to rush off in too much of a hurry.

"Type those letters up tomorrow, Susan: don't start them now. And tell young Alec to come up and see me before he goes."

"Yes, Lady Dinnister, of course."

Susan rose to her feet and smiled. She felt quite relaxed now. Lady Dinnister took her hand for a second.

"And if you can't be good, take the pill."

Susan laughed. This time she didn't feel embarrassed at all. "Very well," she said. "I'll remember." And she turned and went out of the room.

Lady Dinnister renewed her scrutiny of the television set.

Miss Fosdyke took off her glasses and held them against her chin reflectively. "You're very hard on that girl, you know," she said after a moment.

"Nonsense."

"Oh yes, you are. She's a very sensitive young woman."

"I know — that's why I do it. She's too thin-skinned by half, and she must learn to take a few knocks. And anyway, why are you defending her all of a sudden? You've no time for the girl yourself."

"Oh, what an outrageous thing to say," said Miss Fosdyke. The words were strong, but her tone indicated that in fact she was not greatly offended. "She's a perfectly charming young woman."

"Maybe, but you don't approve of her liaison with my grandson."

"Ah, well now, that's an entirely different matter," acknowledged Miss Fosdyke.

"So you admit it then — you don't approve, do you?"

"I've never said so."

"I know that, dammit, but do you or don't you?"

"Language, language," said Miss Fosdyke soothingly. "But, since you ask, no, I don't approve. I don't think they should get quite so involved with each other."

"Why not?"

"Well, because Susan is twenty-four, and Alec is only twenty."

"Good grief, what's that got to do with it? It's all the rage these days, young men and older women. I'm expecting to be proposed to myself any day now."

"It may be all the rage," said Miss Fosdyke primly, "but that doesn't mean that it's right. And in any case, that's not the main problem."

"What is then?"

"Alec still hasn't finished at university yet, so he's in no position to think about getting married."

"And?" said Lady Dinnister, sensing that there was more.

"Well, fundamentally," said Miss Fosdyke grudgingly, "fundamentally, of course, they come from different classes of society."

"Different classes?" squawked Lady Dinnister. "Different classes? Good grief, I haven't heard the word 'class' mentioned for about fifteen years."

"The social classes exist, nonetheless."

"Well, strap me." said Lady Dinnister, apparently made quite speechless by Miss Fosdyke's attitude.

"It would not be a good match," persisted Miss Fosdyke, who in her time had had the better of much fiercer opponents in debate than Lady Dinnister. "And, what's more, I told her so."

"Oh, you did, did you?"

"Yes."

"What, uninvited?"

"Certainly not." Miss Fosdyke's shoulders twitched at the very suggestion. "She asked my advice, in confidence."

"So you told her that you didn't think they would make a good pair?"

"Yes. For the reasons that I've outlined, and for other reasons too."

"Oh — and what did she say to that?"

"She said that she loved him, and she didn't care who knew it."

"Good for her!" Lady Dinnister hooted with laughter. Then she folded her hands in her lap with an eminently satisfied expression on her face.

"What in heaven's name did she ask you for, anyway? Since when have you been any sort of an expert on love?"

Miss Fosdyke was hurt but not offended. In her working life as a hospital almoner, she had been exposed to an unending stream of unjustified criticism, and over the years she had been called things that even sergeant-majors had never heard of; a slight on her spinsterhood was a mere pinprick by comparison.

"Oh, you'd be surprised what I know about love," she said calmly. "Forty years in a hospital teach you a great deal about human nature, and some people — not all, of course — but some people can recognise my expertise. And, in any case, I was once engaged myself, you know."

Lady Dinnister was genuinely surprised. "Oh? When?"

"Well, unofficially engaged, I suppose I should say. It was during the war, and he was killed before we could make it formal."

"Oh." Lady Dinnister's mouth hardened, as if she had remembered something painful. "Well, I'm sorry to hear that, Emily, very sorry. But we all lost men in the war."

"It's not that I'm unsympathetic to young lovers," said Miss Fosdyke, picking up her book and finding her place again. "Far from it. But, having seen so many marriages go wrong, I'm quite convinced that people should get it right in the first place. The right person, the right class, and the right age."

*

Susan Green, notebook and pencil in hand, made her way rapidly down the stairs. Every morning when she awoke she told herself that today she would adopt a more mature approach. Today she would become more adult in her emotions; she would not let her heart beat frantically at the mere sound of Alec Bannerman's motorbike, and she would not rush headlong from wherever she was at the time to greet him.

So much for good intentions and resolutions made over breakfast. Now, when put to the test, here she was, just as breathless and just as excited as ever.

Susan's long legs stepped out vigorously as she crossed the hall, her notebook clutched to her chest with both hands. The door to her office was open, and she turned into it, her eyes shining, her cheeks glowing. She was fairly certain that she looked ridiculously happy and adoring, but she didn't care. That was the way she felt.

"Oh, hello, Alec," she said, as if his presence were unexpected.

Alec Bannerman looked up from the chair behind the desk and smiled, almost lazily. "Hello, Sue." he said. He swung his legs down from the top of the desk, came round, and kissed her gently on the cheek. "How's things?"

Susan smiled, glanced downwards, and fiddled with her pencil, as if looking him straight in the eye were more than she could cope with. "Oh, fine. Just fine," she said.

Alec moved away from her and sat down in another chair beside the filing cabinets. "Are you finished for the day?"

"Mm, yes, yes, I think so. I've just taken a whole lot of dictation from your grandmother, but it can wait till tomorrow to be typed up."

"Good. Because I was wondering if you'd like to go for a little walk."

Susan's pulse rate began to rise alarmingly. She put her notebook and pencil down on the desk as calmly as she could. "Well, yes," she said. "It's a lovely warm day. Why not?"

A few minutes later the pair of them left the house by the back door and began to walk across the gently sloping lawn toward the lake and the summerhouse. Beyond the lake, which was about half a mile long and a quarter of a mile wide, lay a small wood; the wood was full of shade, long grass, and discreet hollows. Further away still, behind a high wall, lay a road.

Alec led the way. He was twenty years old, six-feet-two-inches tall, with a slim but muscular physique. He was wearing a pair of casual cord trousers and a sports shirt open nearly to the waist, revealing what was for an Englishman a surprisingly deep tan. In the eyes of most women, and not just Susan Green, he was quite breathtakingly handsome, but unlike most young men in that position, he seemed quite unconscious of his good looks and made no attempt to exploit them.

Susan held his hand as they walked. For the most part she said nothing, quite content to enjoy the pleasure of stealing an occasional glance at his profile.

"I can't stay long, I'm afraid," said Alec.

"Oh — why not?"

"Well, we've got a sort of family gathering — some sort of financial discussion."

"Oh." Susan wondered if she should ask what the discussion was about, but it was none of her business and, in any case, she wasn't interested.

"Yes," Alec continued. "I suspect Elizabeth and her husband are going to have another go at persuading my father and me to go along with the idea they've raised before."

"What — the idea of getting your grandmother to sell Marlby Manor?"

"Yes."

They reached the edge of the lake and began to walk round its eastern end, across a small footbridge, toward the wood.

"Your brother-in-law was here yesterday. While Lady Dinnister was out for a drive."

"Oh?"

"Yes. Hazel told me. He was showing someone round."

"Trust him," said Alec grimly. "Probably a potential buyer."

They crossed the footbridge.

"Would it really save money if she sold the manor now?" asked Susan.

"Probably," said Alec. "So I understand, anyway. If she sells the place now, passes on the money to Elizabeth and me, and then lives for a certain number of years, I gather that there will be some tax advantages."

"Oh. I see ... Do you think she should do that?"

"No, not really. My father and I think she shouldn't do it if she doesn't want to."

"And she doesn't want to." Susan stated it as a fact.

"No. I know exactly how she feels. She says the manor and its park are beautiful, and she wants to keep them until she dies."

"Yes, and I don't blame her. They are beautiful, it's true."

Before long Susan and Alec reached the shelter of the wood. They passed in through its cool archway, wandering this way and that until they found a soft, dry bank, well surrounded by cover.

They sat down. Alec took off his shirt; his skin glistened in the gentle light.

Susan Green lay on her back with one leg bent at the knee. Above her, filtered through the leaves of the trees, she could see bright blue sky and white clouds. After a moment Alec appeared above her, and she closed her eyes as his mouth came down and closed over hers. His hands began to unbutton her blouse. Her body moved underneath him, and she almost fainted with pleasure, but he mistook her ecstasy for hesitation.

"Don't you want to?" he asked.

"Oh yes," she said. "Yes, please."

Three

Shortly after seven o'clock. Alec Bannerman said good-bye to Susan, kick-started his motorbike, and began to make his way home.

Home was his father's large, rather ramshackle Victorian house in a village called Hattley, some five miles away. He arrived there at a quarter past seven, fifteen minutes late for the family meeting.

He noticed as soon as he turned into the drive that his sister's and brother-in-law's car, a Rover 3.5 automatic, was parked outside the front door. He felt the bonnet as he passed, and it was nearly cold, indicating that they, at least, had been early.

Alec climbed the three steps to the front door, which was open, and went inside. His father, Edward Bannerman, was waiting in the hall, smoking a cigar right down to its bitter end. Alec wasn't quite sure if his father had come into the hall especially to greet him, or if he had been standing there for some other reason.

"I see they're here then," said Alec without enthusiasm.

Edward grunted, equally unenthusiastic. "Yes. Been here since about a quarter to seven. So far they've drunk the best part of a bottle of gin between them ... Have you had anything to eat?"

"No, not yet. But I'd rather talk first and eat later. What about you?"

"No, I haven't had anything. We'll have something after they've gone."

Alec paused, looking carefully into his father's face. Every day he did the same thing, and every day it seemed that the pain lines were etched a little deeper into the features.

"'Are you okay, Dad?" he asked anxiously.

"Hm? Oh, yes, yes, I'm all right. Nothing wrong with me that time won't cure." Edward grinned. "Come on — let's go and hear them out."

Father and son moved on into the living room, where Elizabeth Hassett, Edward's daughter and Alec's sister, was waiting with her husband, Vernon Hassett.

"Oh, hello there, Alec," said Vernon heartily, coming over to shake hands. "How're you doing?"

"I'm okay," said Alec neutrally. "How are you two?"

"We're very well," said Vernon. "Very well indeed."

Elizabeth said nothing and drew heavily on a Sobranie cigarette. She was sitting with her left hand tucked under her right arm, the cigarette held up close to her mouth, her eyes half-closed against the smoke.

"Would you like a drink, Alec?" asked Edward, standing by the sideboard.

"Er, yes, I'll have a lager, please," said Alec.

Edward gave him one and then sat down facing his son. Elizabeth sat on his right, with her husband opposite. There was a momentary pause.

"Well, Vernon," said Edward. "You asked for this meeting — perhaps you'd better chair it."

"Of course," said Vernon hastily. "Of course." He pushed his black-framed glasses further back on the bridge of his nose and began to speak. His manner was that of a young advertising executive outlining a campaign to a client.

"Well now," Vernon began. "Let's get down to business. The basic situation is, I think, well known to us all. And essentially it's very simple. Lady Dinnister is an extremely wealthy woman. She has enjoyed life, and she has certainly never been mean, but she has a great deal of money left. And she's been surprisingly frank about what she's going to do with it — who she's going to leave it to. What she's said is that, in order to reduce the effect of taxation, she's not going to leave any of it to you, Edward. And that's with your knowledge and agreement. But she is going to leave the bulk of her estate to her two grandchildren, Alec and, er, Elizabeth. Plus, of course, very generous legacies to her various servants, all of whom have also been told what to expect."

Vernon paused and glanced round at his audience. Alec and Edward seemed politely interested, and only his wife looked bored. He ploughed on.

"Now, the problem, of course, lies in death duties — or capital transfer tax, to give it its proper name. Capital transfer tax is designed to reduce large individual holdings of wealth, and however hard you wriggle, it will bite more deeply into what money you leave than estate duty ever did. In the old days you used to be able to hand over all your money to whoever you wanted to get it, and if you lived for a further five years, then there was no tax to pay at all. Nowadays it doesn't work like that, but it is still the case that if a person of substance makes a gift and lives for at least three years, then the effect of capital transfer tax is very much reduced."

My God, thought Alec, *what a pompous prick this man is*. He leaned back, closed his eyes and, for his sister's sake, tried to look as if he were giving the matter the serious attention that it deserved.

"The making of a gift before death," Vernon continued, "is also of very great benefit to those to whom the gifts are made, inasmuch as they are able to use the money right now, instead of having to wait until the person making the gifts actually dies. Not a negligible factor, as I'm sure you'll all agree." Vernon finished his gin-and-tonic, set the glass down beside him, and leaned forward. He was pleased with the way his presentation was going; he had thought about it in great detail and had even rehearsed it in his bedroom the previous day.

"The key factor in all this, of course, is Lady Dinnister's wishes — and she has said on many occasions that she wants to do the very best she can for her grandchildren. Now, given that objective, I am quite convinced that her wisest course of action is to transfer the great bulk of her wealth now, while she's still in good health and has many years of life ahead of her. Her main asset, of course, is the house, Marlby Manor. It's also much the most serious drain on her time and energies and financial resources. In fact, not to put too fine a point on it, it costs her a small fortune to run."

"So you think she should sell it," said Alec, still with his eyes closed.

Vernon paused for a second. "Yes," he said. "I do. I think she should find somewhere smaller, which would be very much easier to run."

"And a lot cheaper, too," said Alec.

"Yes, that's true. She wouldn't need so many servants. But it would be much less of a worry for her; that's the main point. Far less to think about. Now, yesterday afternoon — just between ourselves — I showed a friend of mine around the manor."

"What sort of a friend?" asked Edward, sounding thoroughly alarmed.

"Well, he's an estate agent, as a matter of fact."

"Is he indeed?" said Edward. "I must say, Vernon, l think you had a bit of a cheek doing that."

"Well, somebody around here has got to take the initiative," said Elizabeth sharply. "If it were left to you two, we would never get anywhere."

There was silence for a moment. None of the three men present enjoyed feeling the sharp edge of Elizabeth's tongue, but neither Edward nor Alec wanted to start a dogfight, so they let the comment pass.

Vernon looked down at his hands with an expression that indicated that he rather agreed with his wife.

"Well," he said, "it's done now anyway, for better or for worse. Lady Dinnister was out, in any case, so she can't take offence. The point is, my friend assured me that in the current state of the market there would be no difficulty whatever in selling Marlby Manor. No difficulty at all."

"How much would it fetch?" asked Alec.

"About half a million pounds. Not a penny less."

Alec nodded slowly.

"As a matter of fact," Vernon continued, "my friend has even got a buyer in mind. An Arab. The manor has a great deal going for it, you know — a wall all the way round, good main gates, good security. You could land a helicopter on the front lawn with no trouble at all. Possibly fit in a short airstrip if you really tried."

"I think we'd better know what you're proposing," said Edward. His cigar was finished, and he looked around restlessly for his pipe.

Vernon blinked. He had been under the impression that he was getting to the point with almost indecent haste as it was. "What I'm proposing," he said slowly, " — what Elizabeth and I are jointly proposing — is that Lady Dinnister should be persuaded to sell Marlby Manor as soon as possible. She should then, as I say, buy somewhere much smaller, which would not require so much effort to look after, or so many staff to service. She would still need help in the house, of course — quite a lot of it — but she would not have the massive bills for maintenance, rates, and heating and whatnot. She could then rationalise her portfolio, set aside ample funds to keep her in very comfortable circumstances for the rest of her life, even allowing for inflation — "

"And pass on the rest to her grandchildren," Edward finished for him.

"Yes."

"The only trouble with that proposal," said Alec, "is that we've heard it all before. About a year ago. And Grandmother rejected it then."

Elizabeth spoke up again, her voice sharper than ever. "That was different," she said. "Times have changed now. It's time we had another go — persuade her to see sense. She can't go on living in that huge great mansion forever — it's ridiculous. It makes no sense at all." Elizabeth sucked hard on her cigarette, the fingers of her left hand drumming on the arm of her chair.

Edward frowned fiercely; he didn't seem to like the idea one bit. "And if we accept this suggestion," he said cautiously, "who's to do the persuading?"

"I think it would be best if you were to handle that," said Vernon. "You're her son-in-law, you're a member of the family, and yet you're remote, objective. You have no personal axe to grind."

"My two children stand to benefit a great deal," said Edward. "I'd hardly call that not having an axe to grind." Vernon did not answer the point but turned to Alec instead. "Well, Alec, what do you think?"

"As I said before, it's been suggested already and rejected."

"I acknowledge that, but is it a sound and rational proposal?"

Alec paused for a moment and then sighed. "Well, yes," he said reluctantly. "If you look at it in purely financial terms, I suppose it is."

Vernon turned back to his father-in-law. "Well, Edward — is this something you're prepared to support or not?"

Before answering, Edward crossed the room to pick up his pipe and tobacco pouch. He sat filling his pipe as he spoke. "Well," he said slowly, "in the old days I used to think that money was not important. That was rubbish, of course; it's very important indeed. I think it was Somerset Maugham who said that money is the sixth sense that enables you to make full use of the other five … So I agree in principle that this suggestion is a very sensible one. My only worry is on the emotional side of all this. Let's suppose for a moment that Lady Dinnister agreed to go through with it, as you've suggested. I have a nasty feeling that once she saw the old house being sold, she might be absolutely heartbroken. In fact, it might even precipitate her death. I wouldn't want to do anything that would shorten the old girl's days and, in any case, it would negate the whole purpose of the exercise because then you'd have to pay just as much tax as if she held onto everything until she died."

"She shows every sign of living to be a hundred," said Elizabeth firmly. "There are times when I think she'll live a damned sight longer than I will, and I'm quite sure that selling the house wouldn't shorten her life by one day."

Edward glanced across at his son. "Well, Alec?"

Alec leaned forward and sighed. "I suppose we've got to be realistic," he said sadly. "Marlby Manor *is* far too big and ridiculously expensive to run. I suppose Grandmother can afford it, more or less, but none of us would ever want to live there … So I suppose this idea ought to be put to her." He looked down at the floor, apparently rather depressed.

Edward took his pipe out of his mouth. "Very well," he said, though without much enthusiasm. "If that's what you want, I'll do it."

Four

Halfway through the following afternoon, rain stopped play in the cricket match being shown on television, so Lady Dinnister changed channels on her Grundig twenty-six-inch set and watched the horse racing instead. In her youth she had been a keen rider and at one time or another had attended most of the classic races; when the fancy took her, she was also a fearless gambler.

After watching the jockeys mounting the runners in the four-twenty race at Bath, she picked up the *Daily Telegraph* and asked Miss Fosdyke to ring down for Tanner.

He arrived about a minute later, panting slightly from the exertion of mounting the stairs. He was short and stout, and sixty-four years old, so stairs were beginning to become something of a problem to him. He had dropped frequent hints that Lady Dinnister would, he was sure, be much more comfortable in one of the downstairs rooms, but so far his employer had steadfastly chosen to ignore him.

"Tanner," said Lady Dinnister thoughtfully, "what do you fancy in the four-twenty at Bath?"

"Birdbrain," said Tanner promptly, without even pausing to think. "Came second last time out at Epsom, and they're offering eight to one."

"Good odds, you think?"

"Excellent, ma'am."

Lady Dinnister put down the *Daily Telegraph* in her lap. "I'll have fifty pounds each way," she said.

There was an immediate snort of surprise and disapproval from Miss Fosdyke. Lady Dinnister turned to look at her.

"Did you say something, Emily?"

"No, no," said Miss Fosdyke airily. "Not a word."

"Was there anything else, ma'am?" asked the butler.

"No thank you. Tanner, that will be all."

"Very good, ma'am," said Tanner. "Oh, I almost forgot. Mr. Edward rang a short time ago while you were having a nap. He asked if he could come round to see you."

"Did he say when?"

"No, ma'am."

"Oh, well, tell him to come after the racing's over."

"Very good, ma'am," said Tanner. He gave a slight bow and then turned and made his way back down the stairs.

You needn't have called me all the way up here for that, he thought to himself bitterly. *We could have said all that on the phone.*

Once in the hall. Tanner switched the telephone through to an outside line and dialed his bookmaker to place the bet. It was a service he performed for Lady Dinnister perhaps a dozen times a year, and what irked him most was that her success rate was a great deal higher than his own.

Upstairs Miss Fosdyke was knitting furiously. Now that the butler had left them, she was also explaining at length why she disapproved of gambling, but Lady Dinnister wasn't listening. As soon as Miss Fosdyke paused, Lady Dinnister spoke about what was uppermost in her mind.

"You know why he's coming, don't you, Emily?" she said.

"Why who's coming?"

"Edward."

"Your son-in-law?"

"Yes."

"No, I can't say I do know."

"He's coming to try to persuade me to sell the manor."

Miss Fosdyke stopped knitting. "Oh, he is, is he?"

"Yes. Young Vernon brought an estate agent round here on Sunday afternoon while we were out. He thinks I don't know about it — but like Joe Frazier, I'm not as dumb as I look."

"Oh," said Miss Fosdyke, slightly nonplussed. "And what are you going to say when Edward puts this idea to you?"

"Wait and see," said Lady Dinnister. "Wait and see."

A few minutes later Birdbrain came in second at six to one, thus yielding a modest profit for both Mr. Tanner and his employer.

*

At six o'clock Edward Bannerman arrived at the manor in a fifteen-year-old Morris Minor, which he drove not because he couldn't afford anything better but because he liked it. Lady Dinnister greeted him with genuine warmth and gave him a large glass of Scotch with ice.

Edward settled back in a comfortable chair and, after a few preliminaries, stated tactfully that he hadn't just come for a chinwag; he had something important to discuss.

Lady Dinnister smiled. "I know that," she said. "But I'd prefer Miss Fosdyke to stay. I'm getting rather old, you know, and I think I'd like an objective opinion of whatever you've got to put to me."

Edward assented with a nod of the head. "Fair enough," he said. "And objectivity is certainly a rare virtue these days, there's no doubt about that."

Skilfully, Edward then proceeded to outline the case which he had agreed to advocate. Lady Dinnister listened with her eyes closed, her head resting on the back of her chair.

Edward began by pointing out that Lady Dinnister had frequently expressed a wish to do everything possible to help her two grandchildren; for that, as their father, he was deeply grateful. He himself, in his later years, had been fortunate enough to be able to afford to do what he really wanted to do in life, which was to paint; he felt his children were extremely lucky to be able to look forward to the prospect of one day having enough capital to pursue their own ambitions, whatever they might be.

"However," Edward continued, "there are problems, and one of them is this wretched capital transfer tax, which is designed to reduce inherited wealth and apparently does so very effectively. We're also very concerned about Marlby Manor — about the strain it imposes on you, and on your resources."

"What sort of strain?"

"Financial. Physical. Mental."

Lady Dinnister nodded, satisfied with the answer.

"On the whole, those of us who care for you most feel that the time has come for you to consider simplifying your life. Scale things down a bit."

Lady Dinnister opened her eyes and brought her head forward. "You mean, of course, that I should sell Marlby Manor and pass on the proceeds to Elizabeth and Alec now, while I still presumably have a few years to live."

Edward nodded. "That's the gist of it, yes."

Lady Dinnister paused for a moment. "Tell me," she said eventually, "you've obviously thought about all this, Edward, and I trust your judgement. Taking everything into account, is it in the family's interests that I should sell Marlby Manor?"

"Leaving aside sentiment, yes," said Edward.

"And if we include sentiment as a factor?"

"Ah well, only you can speak to that."

"Yes." Lady Dinnister was silent for a minute while she thought the matter over. "Well, Edward," she said suddenly, "you must leave it with me. It needs thinking about."

Edward drained the last of his whisky. "Of course," he said, and rose to go.

Lady Dinnister seized his hand as he bent to kiss her cheek. "And what about you?" she said fiercely. "How are you feeling these days?"

Edward seemed somewhat taken aback. "Oh — fine," he said. "I'm fine."

Lady Dinnister pulled him close and kissed him again. She patted his cheek. "Dear Edward," she said affectionately. "You're too nice a man to be a good liar."

*

"How does he look to you?" asked Lady Dinnister, once Edward's Morris Minor had driven away.

"He seemed pretty fit," said Miss Fosdyke cautiously. "A bit tired perhaps."

"I wish it was only tiredness. He's a sick man, I'm afraid. He has cancer. Dr. Milton told me."

Miss Fosdyke knitted thoughtfully. "You really mustn't assume that cancer is invariably fatal, you know."

"No, I know all that. But in his case it will be."

There was silence for a few minutes, broken only by the click of the knitting needles. Then Lady Dinnister spoke again.

"Well, Emily, what do *you* think I should do?"

"Your son-in-law seemed extremely sincere," said Miss Fosdyke, approaching the matter from a very oblique angle.

Lady Dinnister was slightly irritated. "Yes, but do you think I should sell the house or not?"

Miss Fosdyke stopped knitting for a moment. "Well, it is awfully big … Can you afford it?"

"Yes."

"Do you want to sell it?"

"No."

"Why not?"

"Because I've spent the whole of my adult life here. If I sell it, I shall die."

"I shouldn't bother then," said Miss Fosdyke. "Stay here and live to be ninety-nine if that's the way you feel."

Lady Dinnister sighed. "Unfortunately, it's not that simple. I have a duty to the people who come after me ... You've met Elizabeth and her husband — what do you think of them? Objectively, now."

This task gave Miss Fosdyke no trouble; she barely missed a stitch. "Well, Elizabeth has been spoilt, of course. She's a very selfish girl, and I expect her father's to blame for that. As for her husband, well, he's ambitious but not really bright enough to achieve anything."

"They certainly have a mighty extravagant lifestyle," said Lady Dinnister. "Of course, it's nothing compared with how we lived in the old days, but for a young couple these days, with no obvious means of support other than the husband's salary ... Well, I don't know how they do it."

"It's all done by credit card, that's how," said Miss Fosdyke with a sniff.

"Yes, no doubt you're right ... And what about my grandson Alec, what do you think of him?"

"He's young. Very young. And too inexperienced. 'Malleable' I think is the word — malleable in other people's hands."

"And what do you think of me?" asked Lady Dinnister.

"I think you ask too many questions," said Miss Fosdyke firmly.

Her employer laughed. "Well, maybe I do at that. But an awful lot of people depend on me, and they're all wondering what I'm going to do. And it's not just the family I've got to consider; I have employees to think about, too. If I give up Marlby Manor, what will become of Tanner and Hazel, and all the rest of them?"

"Oh, for goodness sake!" said Miss Fosdyke in shocked tones. "That should be the least of your worries. Mr. Tanner will be drawing his pension before long, and all the rest of them would get jobs somewhere else, I should imagine."

"Well, maybe they would and maybe they wouldn't. It's not always so easy … But if it were your decision to make, what would you do? Would you sell the manor or keep it?"

"Keep it," said Miss Fosdyke without hesitation. "Keep it, definitely."

Lady Dinnister closed her eyes and leaned her head backwards again. "Well now, that's all I need," she said sadly. "Conflicting advice."

Five

At five o'clock the following afternoon, Vernon Hassett knocked on the kitchen door at the rear of Marlby Manor. Hazel Quinn, the cook and housekeeper, let him in.

"Oh," she said. "It's you."

Vernon was very full of himself. "Yes, that's right, darling, it's me," he confirmed cheerfully. He reached out and tried to pinch Hazel's ample bottom, but she avoided him with an ease borne of frequent practice.

"Just remember the rules," said Hazel sharply. "You can look, but you can't touch."

"Yes, yes, I know," said Vernon with a heavy sigh. "And what a feast for the eyes you are, my dear."

Not many men would have disagreed with Vernon in that assessment. Hazel Quinn was now thirty-nine years old and, in all respects save one, she was as handsome and attractive a woman as could be found in the county. She was of average height, and a little heavier than average, but the weight was carried in all the right places. She had always been a big boned girl, and now she was beautifully rounded and proportioned, Rubenesque but not flabby, with a particularly spectacular bust. Her curly brown hair was cut short and neat, and her complexion was creamy and clear, with an absolute minimum of makeup. The only flaw in her beauty was in her eyes, which had been hopelessly crossed since childhood. She wore thick-lensed glasses, which disguised the affliction somewhat, and in her calendar-girl days she had always posed with her eyes suggestively hooded. But even with her glasses on, and her eyes wide open, there was still more than enough of Hazel, discreetly but generously displayed, to attract all but the most finicky of men. Most men, in fact, thought she was a knockout.

Vernon stood and gazed at her, his hands on his hips and a distressingly vulgar leer on his face. Hazel did not allow it to stay there long.

"Well, Vernon," she said abruptly, "what brings you here? You haven't come all this way just to stare at me — or if you have, I'll ask you to pay for the privilege." She moved back towards the sink and continued preparing dinner.

"No," said Vernon sadly. "No, you're quite right, Hazel, I haven't come here just to see you. Lady Dinnister sent for me."

"Oh, why?"

"Because she's got some news for me."

"Oh?" Hazel began slicing vegetables on a board. Her back was to Vernon, and he wondered briefly if he dared creep up behind her and give her a quick squeeze. He would dearly have loved to, but the sight of that flashing knife put him off. Instead he went on talking.

"Yes, very good news," he continued. "Such good news that I'd really like to celebrate by taking some more photographs of you."

Hazel turned to look at him through her heavy glasses. She seemed surprised. "Oh — really?"

"Yes. Really. I've got a new camera."

"What, another one?"

"Yes, another one ... Well — what do you say?" He held his breath and was rather disturbed to find that his heart was beating twice as fast as usual.

"Well ... " said Hazel doubtfully. "It'll cost you."

"Of course."

"We've got raging bloody inflation. It'll be seventy-five pounds this time."

"For an hour?"

"For an hour."

Vernon bit his lip. The price was steep, but Hazel was a professional and never tried to cut the time short. He made a decision: it was worth it.

"Okay, then. What about Friday?"

"Afternoon?" asked Hazel.

"Yes. Say four o'clock?"

"Four o'clock. By the summerhouse."

"Yes, fair enough." Vernon relaxed at last, full of smiles again. "Well, that's settled then. I'll look forward to it."

"Just make sure you bring the cash," said Hazel.

"Don't worry," Vernon assured her on his way through the door which led to the hall. "I will."

Vernon departed, closing the kitchen door behind him. Almost at once the back door opened and Lady Dinnister's chauffeur, Len Jones, came in from the yard at the back of the house. He was a tall, heavily built young man with fair hair and blue eyes; he did not look at all pleased.

"Oh, so he's here again, is he?" he grunted.

Hazel made no reply but busied herself with the vegetables. "What did he want this time?"

"He's come to see Lady Dinnister."

"Yes, I know that," said Jones darkly. "But what did he want with you?"

Hazel shrugged. "Oh, the usual."

"Photos again?"

"Yes." Hazel turned to look at the chauffeur, drying her hands on a towel. She grinned at him. "Do you mind?"

Jones smiled back, his anger softened by her manner. "No," he said, "not really. He won't give you any trouble. But make the bugger pay, that's all."

"Don't worry," said Hazel happily. "I will."

*

Vernon Hassett was whistling cheerfully as he climbed the stairs to Lady Dinnister's sitting room. He had, in his view, every reason to feel cheerful. Lady Dinnister had phoned him at work early that afternoon, asking him to call in on his way home, as she wanted to discuss "this business of selling the manor" with him. Well, a nod was as good as a wink to Vernon. It sounded to him as if, at long last, his status as the only member of the family who knew anything about financial affairs was being recognised.

He could not have been more mistaken.

Lady Dinnister received him alone and did not ask him to sit down, which was an unprecedented step on her part. Even then poor Vernon did not understand the situation; it was not until he began to be torn into little pieces and sprinkled all over the carpet that he really understood.

"I know your kind, Vernon," Lady Dinnister told him coldly. "I made certain enquiries about you when you became engaged to my granddaughter. I didn't like what I heard then, and I haven't heard anything to change my mind about you since. You were unpopular at school, which doesn't surprise me, and your academic record was abysmal. You got at least one girl pregnant before you latched onto Elizabeth, and apart from paying for the inevitable abortion, you showed no concern for her whatever. So far as I can see, your chief interest in Elizabeth was financial, but she seemed to be genuinely fond of you, so I let the marriage proceed. In short, Vernon, I dislike you. That in itself would not matter very much, provided you behaved in a civilised manner. But you don't. Last Sunday you brought an estate agent round this house without my permission, while I was out, valuing the place as if I were dead already. That I will not stand for. Furthermore, on at least two occasions you have tried to poke your nose into my financial affairs, which are none of your business whatever. You persuaded your father-in-law to act as your spokesman, but the logic of the argument has your stamp all over it. Edward would never dream up a scheme like that, never in a thousand years. You want me to sell the manor and give you half of the proceeds. Well, I am not going to sell it — not now or at any time in the future. I shall stay here until I die."

Lady Dinnister had finished, but for a moment or two Vernon didn't quite appreciate that fact. It had all happened so fast. He just stood there, white-faced and lightly trembling.

"You may go now," Lady Dinnister told him, and with a jerk Vernon came to his senses. He began to walk painfully out of the room. As he reached the door, the old lady called out to him.

"Vernon … "

He turned again to face her.

"Don't worry," said Lady Dinnister with half a smile. "I won't change my will. You'll just have to wait, that's all."

*

Vernon Hassett did not retrace his steps through the kitchen; almost instinctively, he left by the front door and made his way round to the side of the house where he had left his car.

He wasn't quite sure how he felt now: rather stunned, really. He hadn't been spoken to like that since his housemaster had found his collection of *Penthouse* magazines at school. Well, today's session had not been a very happy experience, but then it hadn't been the end of the world either. Just a ticking off, that's all. A bit worse than most. It had happened many times before and would no doubt happen again.

By the time Vernon slumped into the driving seat of his Rover, he had become quite philosophical. Okay, so the old lady hadn't accepted the argument — she'd turned it down flat, in fact — but there was always another day. And she couldn't live forever, when all was said and done. Yes, there was at least that to look forward to.

After a few minutes' pause to collect himself, Vernon drove to his father-in-law's house in Hattley, where he had arranged to meet his wife and to report back to Edward and Alec on what Lady Dinnister had said to him.

"Well?" said Elizabeth sharply, almost as soon as Vernon came into the living room. "What did she say?"

By that time Vernon had recovered all his considerable aplomb; he had not taken his company's middle-management training course for nothing. "I think I'd like a drink please," he said, and would not be drawn out until it had been served.

However, once armed with one of Edward's largest gin-and-tonics, Vernon began to expound on his meeting with Lady Dinnister. He paced up and down in his best managing-director manner.

"Well, friends," he said philosophically, "I'm afraid the answer's no."

"No? What do you mean, no?" Elizabeth squawked at him.

"Just that," said Vernon simply. "She's rejected all our proposals."

"Oh no," said Elizabeth faintly. She bent forward and rocked gently to and fro, as if in physical pain.

"What did she say, exactly?" said Edward. He too seemed very shocked. Only Alec was unsurprised.

"Well … " Vernon paused for thought. "She'd considered our case very carefully, of course, and she acknowledged that there were some powerful arguments on our side. But, when all was said and done, she felt that Marlby Manor was her house, and that she would like to stay there until she dies."

"In about twenty-five years' time," said Elizabeth bitterly.

Her father pursed his lips. "It could hardly be so long," he suggested.

"Oh no? You want to bet?" said Elizabeth loudly. There were tears in her eyes. "She had an old aunt who lived to be a hundred and two. God, it's absolutely sickening. I'd like to kill the old bag myself."

"Now that's enough!" said her father sharply. "That's an absolutely disgraceful thing to say about your grandmother. I will not have such things said in my house!"

For a moment Edward seemed quite beside himself with rage, rising to his feet and striding from one end of the room to the other. But then he seemed to recover his composure.

"Well, so that's that then," he said quietly. "Well, we tried, Vernon. You were right to suggest what you did, and you acted from honest motives. You put forward a good case, and I placed it before her as best I could. But she didn't buy it, so that's that."

Alec still said nothing.

Elizabeth drained her drink and put the glass down. There were tearstains on her cheeks. "You blew it, Dad," she said bluntly. "You could have persuaded her, but you didn't." And with that she gathered up her handbag and cigarettes and walked briskly out of the room.

Vernon looked a little embarrassed. After a moment he excused himself and followed Elizabeth out to the car. Edward and Alec were left alone.

Edward walked slowly to the window and watched his daughter and her husband drive away. Alec came and stood at his shoulder.

"Well," said Edward with a sigh. "Perhaps I did make a mess of it. I don't know. It's hard to tell, really."

"Nonsense, Dad," said Alec firmly. "I'm sure you did an admirable job. No, the fact is that Grandmother simply doesn't want to sell the manor. And I don't blame her; I wouldn't want to either, in her position. And you were right to tell Elizabeth off — she's a mighty selfish young woman."

"It was Fosdyke, you know," said Edward thoughtfully. "She was against it — I could tell. She didn't say anything, but I could feel her opposition. What I really ought to have done was to have concentrated on her."

In the Rover, homeward bound, Elizabeth had dried her eyes and, with difficulty, lit a cigarette. After several deep puffs she felt a little more controlled.

"Well," she said in a voice tight with emotion, "what are we going to do now?"

Vernon kept his eyes on the road. He was surprised at his own self-confidence. However hard the blows of fate, he just kept on bouncing back. *Resilient*, he told himself, *that's what I am.*

"Oh, we aren't finished yet," he said aloud.

"Aren't we?" said Elizabeth bitterly. "We can't just go on borrowing and borrowing, you know. Sooner or later they're going to want their money. And what do we do then?"

"Oh, we'll think of something," said Vernon carelessly. "Don't worry. We'll think of something."

Six

On the Thursday of that week, Lady Dinnister and Miss Fosdyke spent the afternoon in Sixton-on-Weal, looking round the antique shops. Miss Fosdyke was, if anything, rather more interested in antiques — particularly porcelain — than was Lady Dinnister, but they both enjoyed poking round in old corners and seeing what they could find. Between them they bought one silver spoon as a present for Miss Fosdyke's sister, and then had tea at a small cafe by the river. After that they decided to go home.

As usual on their joint shopping expeditions, the two ladies were driven by Lady Dinnister's chauffeur, Len Jones. The car he drove was a Rolls-Royce, a limousine-de-ville with a body built by the firm of James Young on a Phantom V chassis. It was a large, elegant car, with a sliding roof over the driver's seat that enabled Jones to enjoy the August sunshine.

Now chauffeurs do not normally expect wheels to come off Rolls-Royces, not even those which are nearly twenty years old. Len Jones certainly didn't expect anything of the kind, which was why he took some time to react when odd things began to happen.

The first thing that happened was that a hideous clattering noise developed. This was followed almost immediately by an unnerving change for the worse in the Rolls's handling characteristics. Jones woke up a bit, grasped the steering wheel tightly, and glanced in the mirror. That, unfortunately, was a mistake because in taking his eyes off the road ahead of him he failed to notice a deep pothole at the side of the quiet country lane. The near-side front wheel of the car, which was causing all the trouble, slumped into the pothole, bounced awkwardly out again, and slewed the car sideways so that both of the off-side wheels settled heavily into the ditch on the right-hand side of the lane.

Both old ladies, in the back seat, were thrown off balance. Miss Fosdyke's weight fell on Lady Dinnister, and she in turn struck her lip on the window-frame. For a moment or two there was some undignified scrambling and several squeaks of surprise and alarm. Almost immediately, however, the two ladies realised that the car had stopped, that they were still in one piece, and that only relatively minor injuries had been sustained.

Jones turned off the engine, leapt out of his driver's seat, and rushed to check that his passengers were unharmed. He pulled open the rear door and looked anxiously into the backseat. "Are you all right, ma'am?" he asked.

Miss Fosdyke pulled herself upright. "Yes. Yes, I think we're all right," she said rather breathlessly. She turned to Lady Dinnister. "What about you, Ann?"

Lady Dinnister put her hand over her mouth; when she removed it, there was blood on her finger. "Oh," she said, "I seem to have cut my lip. How silly."

Miss Fosdyke reacted promptly. She herself was only shaken and, using the car's first-aid kit, she soon stemmed the flow of blood from Lady Dinnister's lip and made suitably sympathetic noises. In the meantime Jones checked over the car.

He realised almost at once that the source of the trouble was loose nuts on the front near-side wheel. He could hardly believe his eyes, but that's what it was; the wheel had begun to work loose, causing the loud clattering noise and the sudden change in the car's handling that had momentarily distracted him.

Cursing violently under his breath, Jones asked the two old ladies if they would be kind enough to get out of the car for a few minutes; he helped them to make themselves comfortable in the shade of a nearby tree. Then he jacked up the car, tightened the loose wheel-nuts, checked all the others, and finally declared the car fit for the rest of the journey.

"Have you found the cause of the trouble?" Lady Dinnister asked nervously.

"Oh yes, I've found the cause of the trouble all right," said Jones savagely. "It's that Mr. Welsh at the garage, that's the cause of the trouble. He had the car in for servicing yesterday, ma'am, and either he or one of his mechanics must have left those wheel-nuts loose. I'll give him a piece of my mind after I've taken you home, don't you worry."

Fifteen minutes later the Rolls-Royce arrived back at Marlby Manor. Lady Dinnister had begun to feel slightly dizzy during this part of the journey, and Jones honked loudly as they drew up outside the front door.

Hazel and Tanner both came running out. Hazel helped Miss Fosdyke to escort Lady Dinnister upstairs, while Tanner tutted disgustedly as the chauffeur described the shortcomings of Mr. Welsh and his mechanics.

Upstairs Miss Fosdyke felt Lady Dinnister's pulse. "I think we'd better send for the doctor," she announced after checking her watch. "You seem to have had rather a nasty shock, and that cut on your lip may need a stitch or two."

Lady Dinnister protested feebly but soon gave up and gratefully closed her eyes. Now that she came to think about it, she really didn't feel too good. Not too good at all.

Dr. Milton arrived an hour later. He too took Lady Dinnister's pulse, decided that the cut on her mouth would manage without a stitch, and declared that an early night would not go amiss.

"Very good, Doctor," said Miss Fosdyke primly, sounding more like a governess than a companion. "Don't you worry, we'll take good care of her."

"I'm sure you will," said Dr. Milton, but his smile looked rather forced.

On his way out Dr. Milton passed Jones and Tanner, who were outside standing by the Rolls-Royce and muttering darkly about the standards of modern workmanship.

"I gather you had a bit of trouble with one of the wheels," Dr. Milton remarked.

"Yes, Doctor, you might say that." said Jones. "Mr. Welsh in the village had the car in for a service yesterday, so I've just been round to ask him why he didn't bother to tighten up the wheel-nuts after he'd finished."

Dr. Milton grinned. "And what did he say to that?"

Jones grunted. "Denied all knowledge of it, of course. Told me he worked on the car himself, double-checked everything, always does."

"Well, he would say that, wouldn't he?" said Tanner. "He could hardly say anything else."

"Ah, well, there's no great harm done," said Dr. Milton, turning to go. "Lady Dinnister will be as right as rain tomorrow. You needn't feel too concerned about it."

The butler and the chauffeur stood and watched Dr. Milton drive away, his car sending clouds of dust into the glowing evening air.

"That's not the point, though, is it?" said Jones thoughtfully when the dust had begun to settle.

"What isn't the point?" asked the older man.

"Well, that no great harm's been done. It might have been done; that's the point. Supposing I'd been trundling along at sixty or seventy on the motorway? I can't understand old Welshie making a mistake like that. Until today I'd have trusted him with my life."

"Yes," said Tanner. "I'm inclined to agree with you. As garages go, he has a pretty good reputation."

"You know what he said?" asked Jones rhetorically.

"No, what did he say?"

Jones put on his most outraged and offended expression. "He said if the nuts on that wheel were loose, it could only have been because someone had done it deliberately! Now I ask you — is that likely?"

Seven

Shortly before four o'clock the following afternoon, Hazel took Lady Dinnister a pot of tea and a piece of cake; Lady Dinnister, as usual, was in her sitting room upstairs.

"How's your lip feeling?" asked Hazel.

"Oh, perfectly all right," said Lady Dinnister. "Perfectly all right." Then something caught her attention; she put down her book, took off her reading glasses, and looked at her housekeeper carefully.

"Hazel … "

"Yes, Lady Dinnister?"

"Why aren't you wearing a bra?"

Hazel laughed, genuinely amused. "Well, because it's a very warm day," she said. "Too warm to wear anything, really."

"Oh yes, I see," said Lady Dinnister doubtfully. "Well, it'll be a damn sight warmer if you let any men see you walking around like that. Miss Fosdyke wouldn't approve at all."

"No," said Hazel, "I don't suppose she would." The tone of her voice indicated that she was not too worried about what Miss Fosdyke thought. "And, speaking of Miss Fosdyke, will she be in to dinner?"

"Oh no. No, I'm sorry, Hazel, I should have told you earlier. She's gone to have tea with a friend, and then she's got a meeting of one of her museum committees, so she won't be back until later."

"Oh, right," said Hazel. "Well, if you don't mind, I think I'll go for a short walk before starting the cooking. Will that be all right?"

"Yes. Yes, of course," said Lady Dinnister. "Is Susan still here?"

"Yes, she's just typing some letters. Mr. Tanner's in his room, and Len is doing a bit of painting out the back."

"Oh well, there's plenty of help around then. I shan't come to any harm. Where are you going to?"

"Oh, just over to the far side of the lake."

Lady Dinnister glanced towards the window. "Well, take your time," she said with a sigh. "I'd come with you, but I'm afraid my days for walking any distance are over."

Shortly afterwards, Hazel disappeared downstairs, and Lady Dinnister continued reading for a while. But then, suddenly, a thought struck her. She stood up and pushed her chair round so that she could comfortably see out of the window overlooking the lake. Then she opened a cupboard at knee height, reached in, and pulled out a pair of 8 x 40 binoculars.

*

At four o'clock sharp, Vernon Hassett arrived for his photography session with Hazel. He parked his Rover just inside the north gate, well out of sight of the manor, and walked southwest across the park toward the summerhouse. By the time he reached it, he was sweating heavily, despite having left the jacket of his suit in the car.

As agreed, Hazel was sitting in the cool interior of the summerhouse waiting for him. "Hello, Vernon." she said cheerfully, as his shadow fell across the entrance.

He gave her a nervous smile. "Hello, Hazel. How's things?"

"All right."

"Hot, isn't it?" suggested Vernon, wiping his brow.

"Yes," said Hazel. "Stifling."

There was a pause for a moment or two; Vernon found the silence more worrying than Hazel.

"Well," he said eventually, "shall we go then?"

Hazel smiled at him directly in reply. "Let's pay first, shall we?" she suggested.

"Oh. Oh yes, of course." Vernon reached into the back pocket of his trousers and took out his wallet. He extracted a handful of five-pound notes and counted fifteen of them onto the aged wooden table in front of him. "There," he said. "All right?"

"Yes, that's right," said Hazel. She picked up the seventy-five pounds and tucked them into a crack in the wall behind her.

"Will it be safe there?" asked Vernon doubtfully.

"Oh yes. I'll collect it on the way back." Hazel smiled again. "Come on then, let's go."

Together Hazel and Vernon left the summerhouse and walked north, away from the manor. Vernon gave one nervous glance backwards to check that no one was watching them and then seemed to relax. Hazel appeared quite untroubled by anything. They crossed a wooden footbridge over the stream which fed the lake and then turned left and entered the wood. It was cooler among the trees, the intense heat of the sunlight being filtered through leaves and branches.

Hazel led the way until they reached a small clearing among the trees. There was still plenty of shade, but the undergrowth thinned out, leaving soft grass underfoot. Anyone who was sufficiently observant could just see the upper floors of the manor, to the south. But Vernon was not very observant. He was interested only in what was close at hand, not in those things which were some distance away.

"Here," said Hazel. "I think this should do."

"Yeah," said Vernon eagerly. He unfastened the leather case of his brand-new Canon A-1 single-lens reflex and began to squint through the eyepiece.

Hazel had a contented smile on her face. She hummed a happy tune as she began to unbutton the front of her dress. When it was open all the way down the front, she spread it sideways and slipped both arms out of the sleeves simultaneously.

As Lady Dinnister had remarked earlier, Hazel was not wearing a bra. She wasn't wearing anything else, either.

Vernon found his breath constricted. This was not the first time he had seen Hazel nude — not by a long way — but her figure never ceased to amaze him. He had first seen photographs of Hazel in the nudist magazines that he and his friends had studied so eagerly at school; in later years he had often seen her on calendars and in occasional bit parts in films. But nothing — no photograph, and not even Hazel clothed — nothing had prepared him for the impact of Hazel naked in the flesh.

She was heavily voluptuous in a manner which surpassed Vernon's wildest imaginings. Her bust was so large that it looked as if it ought to drop about six inches when she took her bra off. But it didn't; it stayed exactly where it was Just as well shaped as ever — which was why Hazel's career as a photographic model had always been so successful.

Hazel stretched her arms upward and flexed her muscles, relaxing in the cool of the shade.

Small beads of sweat appeared on Vernon's upper lip.

"How's this?" asked Hazel, asking about both her position under the tree and her pose.

"Fine, fine. Great," said Vernon, gulping once or twice. "But the — um — the glasses?"

"Oh. Oh yes," said Hazel. And with a final glance to check that the manor was still visible behind her, she took off her glasses and deposited them carefully on top of her dress.

The world became pleasantly fuzzy.

*

Hazel made a salad for dinner, followed by cheese and biscuits. Most of the salad had been grown in the manor garden, which Lady Dinnister said made all the difference.

Lady Dinnister ate dinner in her sitting room, and she asked Hazel to keep her company. Miss Fosdyke was out, Susan Green had gone home, and Lady Dinnister did not fancy eating alone. So the two women had their meal upstairs while Tanner and Jones talked sport together in the kitchen.

Hazel served coffee afterwards, and Lady Dinnister was thoughtful as she stirred a spoonful of sugar into her cup. "By the way," she said quietly, "I saw Master Vernon on the grounds this afternoon."

"Oh yes," said Hazel calmly. "He was here."

Lady Dinnister glanced at her sideways. "I didn't know he was interested in photography."

"Oh yes," said Hazel again. "Dead keen."

Lady Dinnister tasted her coffee. "Pays you, does he?"

"Oh yes."

"Good." The old lady nodded. "So that's why you weren't wearing a bra — so there wouldn't be any marks on your skin."

"Yes," said Hazel. Then she turned to look at her employer with a smile. "How did you know about that?"

Lady Dinnister laughed. "Oh, through having an artist for a son-in-law, that's how. I used to go and see Edward sometimes, and he'd be painting a nude, and once or twice he complained bitterly about the marks of elastic all over his models. Though why it should bother him I don't quite know; it wasn't as if he were photographing them. But I think it put him off somehow. Spoilt his idea of perfection. He's painted some excellent nudes over the years. Perhaps I should get him to show them to you sometime?"

"Thank you," said Hazel simply. "But I think I've already seen most of them."

"Oh," said Lady Dinnister. She sounded surprised but said nothing more.

When they had finished their coffee, Hazel gathered together the dirty plates and placed them on a tray.

"Would you do me a favour, Hazel?" asked Lady Dinnister.

"Of course."

"When you've finished the washing-up, would you be kind enough to come back and wash my hair?"

"Yes, certainly," said Hazel. "I won't be long."

Fifty minutes later both the washing-up and the hair washing were complete. Lady Dinnister's visits to the hairdresser were growing less frequent with advancing age and were now down to about one a month. But she liked having her hair washed perhaps twice a week, and Miss Fosdyke usually obliged. Tonight, however, it was Hazel's turn, and when Lady Dinnister was sitting comfortably with a towel around her shoulders, Hazel picked up the hair-dryer and plugged it into a socket.

As she did so, she gave a loud, startled scream. She dropped the hair-dryer with a crash, and clutched her right wrist with her left hand, in obvious pain and distress.

"Hazel!" cried Lady Dinnister in alarm. She struggled to her feet. "Whatever happened? Are you all right?"

Hazel's face had been momentarily as white as the towel around Lady Dinnister's shoulders; but now the blood flooded back, and she went rather pink, swaying on her feet.

"Yes, yes, I think I'm all right. But I'd better sit down for a minute."

Hazel sat down heavily on the nearest chair, still clutching her right hand. Lady Dinnister clucked around her sympathetically.

"My dear Hazel, whatever happened to you?"

"It was the dryer," said Hazel weakly. "I plugged it in and it gave me a shock — a really bad one."

"Oh my goodness me, you might have been electrocuted!"

"Yes," said Hazel weakly. "I know. Two hundred and forty volts is no joke."

Help was summoned from below in the shape of Alfred Tanner and Len Jones. Brandy was administered to Hazel, and the two men, under Lady Dinnister's close supervision, investigated the source of the electric shock.

The hair-dryer was a distinctly older model with a chrome metal case and a rubber handle. It was noisy but powerful and normally very effective; up to the present it had given years of useful service. Len took it apart with a screwdriver, and when it was opened up, Lady Dinnister scrutinised it carefully through her reading glasses.

"There — see?" she asked triumphantly, pointing with her painfully arthritic forefinger. "There's a bare wire, there, do you see?"

"Yes," said Len. "That's what did it, all right."

Lady Dinnister turned to Hazel. "There's a bare wire touching the side of the case, my dear. That's what gave you the shock. Now how would a thing like that happen?"

Len Jones scratched his head. "Well, it must have worn through, that's all. You must have had it a good many years, ma'am."

"But how could it have worn through?" demanded Lady Dinnister angrily. "There are no moving parts in there; there's nothing for it to wear out against."

The two men said nothing. Hazel sipped her brandy; she was still white and visibly trembling, and she didn't like to think what a close shave she'd had.

Lady Dinnister's mouth set into a hard, thin line. "It looks to me," she said, "as if the covering on that wire has been scraped off deliberately."

For a moment no one said anything, but then Tanner broke the shocked silence. "Surely not, ma'am," he said gently. "Who would do a thing like that?"

Lady Dinnister did not reply, but she glanced from face to face. "First of all," she said grimly, "I get my hand pierced by a nasty piece of dirty wire on a bouquet. Then a wheel nearly comes off my car. And now poor Hazel has had a dreadful electric shock."

There was a pause. Then Lady Dinnister continued.

"You know," she said, "if I were not such a level-headed and sensible old lady, I might get the impression that someone was trying to kill me."

And behind the rounded lenses of her glasses, Hazel's eyes opened wide.

Eight

Hazel Quinn had always been an early riser, particularly in the summer, and particularly at Marlby Manor, where her bedroom window faced east. Her living quarters were on the upper floor of the former stable block at the rear of the main house.

On Tuesday August the twenty-eighth, Hazel was awake at 6:00 A.M. She glanced at the alarm clock and realised that there was no need for her to get up for at least another hour. With a happy sigh, she turned over on her side and snuggled closer to the long, muscular frame of Len Jones beside her in the bed. Len was not an early riser by any stretch of the imagination, but given repeated prods in the ribs accompanied by frequent blowing in his ear, he could sometimes be made semi-conscious by about half past six. That was the case on this occasion.

By 6:45 A.M. Len Jones was wide awake and responding enthusiastically to Hazel's kisses. And five minutes later their large double bed was vibrating violently in a manner which threatened to do serious harm to the fabric of the building. In the room immediately below their bedroom, some flakes of loose paint drifted slowly down from the ceiling.

Hazel arose shortly after seven, feeling much refreshed. She had a quick shower, dressed, and crossed the courtyard to the manor.

Inside the kitchen, Tanner had already put the kettle on, and before long a large pot of tea had been brewed. As usual, Hazel took two cups of tea upstairs on a tray. First she entered Lady Dinnister's bedroom.

Lady Dinnister was already awake, and as Hazel entered she sat up, pulled her pillows upright, and made herself comfortable. Hazel drew the curtains, deposited one cup of tea by the bed, and made a few comments on the weather. Then she went along the corridor to Miss Fosdyke's bedroom.

Here she repeated the procedure. She knocked, went into the darkened room, and put down her tray on the bedside table. As she did so, she glanced at the familiar form of Miss Fosdyke, who was lying flat on her back.

In the half-light filtering through the thick, heavy curtains, Miss Fosdyke's eyes stared upwards. Motionless.

Hazel's legs began to tremble.

There was, Hazel realised, an unpleasant smell in the room: a smell of vomit or diarrhea, or possibly both. The door to the adjoining bathroom was open, and the smell came chiefly from there, but also from the bed itself.

"Oh my God!" said Hazel. Her heart began to pound in the most alarming manner.

She took a deep breath and stepped away from the bed. Moving very carefully, she turned around and crossed to one of the two windows. She drew the curtains open, and then, very slowly, willed herself to look back at the bed.

"Oh my God!" said Hazel again.

Moving with extreme caution, so as not to trip over her own feet in panic, Hazel retraced her steps to the kitchen. Tanner was seated at the kitchen table, fully dressed, sipping a mug of tea.

Hazel paused at the door. "Alfred," she said.

Tanner looked up at her.

"It's Miss Fosdyke," said Hazel weakly.

"What about Miss Fosdyke?"

"I think she's dead."

"Dead?" said Tanner.

"Dead," Hazel repeated.

The butler went up the stairs rather faster than usual, and with considerably less dignity than was his norm. When he came down again, his face was nearly as white as his shirt.

"You're right," he said shortly. "She is dead." He sat down heavily. "What are we going to do?"

By this time Hazel had recovered her nerve. "You phone the doctor," she said crisply, "and I'll go and tell Lady Dinnister."

"All right," Tanner said, and tottered off towards the phone.

Hazel returned to Lady Dinnister's bedroom. "Excuse me, ma'am."

Lady Dinnister looked up at her over her teacup. "Yes, Hazel?"

"It's Miss Fosdyke, ma'am. I'm very sorry, but … Mr. Tanner and I think she's dead. She must have died during the night."

After a moment to recover from the shock, Lady Dinnister got out of bed. With Hazel's help, she wrapped herself in a floor-length dressing gown, seized a stout walking stick, and walked with difficulty along the corridor to Miss Fosdyke's bedroom.

She wrinkled her nose as she entered the room but bent closely over the motionless body, and even touched the forehead, leaving her fingers on the skin for some seconds. Then she straightened up with a sigh.

"Yes," she said sadly. "I'm afraid you're right. Have you sent for the doctor?"

"Yes, ma'am."

"Good. Now, please get me a chair from my bedroom and put it outside the door here. Then go downstairs and wait until the doctor comes. Send him straight upstairs when he arrives."

Hazel did as she was told, leaving Lady Dinnister like a guard at the door of Miss Fosdyke's bedroom.

Twenty minutes later Dr. Milton arrived, evidently having dressed in a hurry, and without having shaved. He came upstairs alone, a serious expression on his face.

"Good morning," he said with a nod.

"Good morning," said Lady Dinnister. She leaned on her stick and stood up. Her manner was thoughtful but controlled. "You'd better come inside."

She advanced into the room but moved away from the bed. Dr. Milton followed her and immediately began an examination of Miss Fosdyke. It did not take him long.

After a few moments the doctor dropped his stethoscope back into his bag and straightened up again. "Well, you're right, of course," he said. "I'm sorry to say that Miss Fosdyke certainly is dead, and has been for several hours."

"She was as fit as a fiddle yesterday," said Lady Dinnister in a tone which did not encourage contradiction.

"Maybe so," said the doctor. "But death comes to us all sooner or later — and she was in her sixties."

"She seems to have been sick."

"Yes." Dr. Milton glanced back at the bed. "She seems to have been vomiting fairly heavily."

"Something she ate, do you think?"

"Possibly."

"And it killed her."

"Well, I would suspect that the violent sickness and diarrhea may have precipitated a heart attack. It's difficult to tell for certain." He picked up his bag. "Well, I'll arrange for the body to be removed as soon as I can."

"And you'll arrange for a postmortem too, I hope?" said Lady Dinnister.

Dr. Milton paused at the door. "There almost certainly will be a postmortem, yes. The coroner has to be informed if death may be the result of food poisoning, and that looks to be a possibility in this case."

"And the coroner will order an autopsy?"

"I should imagine he will, yes." Dr. Milton's fingers tapped on the edge of the door. "But why are you so concerned?" he asked.

Lady Dinnister stood up straight and looked him square in the face. "When my friends die," she said grimly, "I like to know why."

Nine

At nine A.M. the following morning, Wednesday the twenty-ninth of August, Detective Chief Superintendent Ben Spence, the head of the Southshire CID, was in his office on the first floor of the Police Headquarters Building in Wellbridge, the county town.

Spence was six feet tall, with a frame which was well covered without a hint of fat. At the age of thirty-nine, he was a handsome and impressive figure of a man, but as a detective it often suited him to be inconspicuous, and he had a knack of looking ordinary and dull when he wished.

He was wearing, as usual, a grey double-breasted suit with long vents on each side at the back and deep, reinforced pockets. His shoes were specially made in London and had been ever since the long days on the beat, many years earlier, had left him with aching feet.

At nine o'clock that morning, Spence was talking to his redheaded colleague, Detective Inspector David Laurel, but they were not, for a change, talking about police business. For the moment the two men were discussing the quality of the fishing on the west coast of Ireland because, in three days' time, Spence was due to start a holiday there.

The chat about fishing was interesting enough, but half of Spence's mind was concentrating on another problem. He had had strict instructions from his wife to find out if Detective Inspector Laurel intended to pursue his acquaintance with an attractive thirty-five-year-old widow, Patricia North, to whom he had been so thoughtfully introduced at a dinner party given by the Spences on the previous Friday night. And Spence was just wondering how he could guide the conversation round to that particular topic when his thoughts were interrupted by a telephone call.

The caller was Dr. Oscar Dunbar, the pathologist appointed to the Southshire Police Force by the Home Office.

"Ben," said Dunbar, without much introduction, "I've got a possible case of poisoning for you. You'd better come on over and have a word about it."

"Oh God," groaned Spence, "you don't mean a murder, do you?"

"Well, I doubt if it's suicide," said Dunbar briskly. "Come on over and I'll tell you more about it."

"Oh, all right," said Spence heavily. "But I hope you're wrong about it being murder. Where are you?"

"Wellbridge General," said Dunbar, and put the phone down.

Spence lowered his own receiver and grinned ruefully at his colleague across the desk. "Here we go again," he said with a sigh. "I have a nasty feeling that my holiday may well have to wait."

*

Twenty minutes later Spence and Laurel found themselves in a small office adjoining the mortuary in Wellbridge General Hospital. Their host, Dr. Oscar Dunbar, was a bald man in his mid-forties with a somewhat military taste in ties and cuff links and an inexhaustible supply of dirty jokes. He told two excruciatingly filthy stories with great enthusiasm and was about to embark on a third when Spence cut him short.

"Oscar," said Spence dourly, "I don't have much time to spare this morning, and I would be greatly obliged if you would save your story for some other time."

Dunbar was not greatly put out. "Oh, all right then, spoilsport," he said cheerfully. "Let's get down to business." He pulled a folder across his desk and opened it. "Now then. Yesterday morning the body of a woman was brought in here. The case had been referred to the coroner by Dr. Milton over at Lower Durwood. Query food poisoning; query possible complications resulting from shock after an accident the week before. In other words, Milton hadn't really got a clue what killed her."

"This woman was from Lower Durwood, you say," Spence broke in.

"No, I didn't say that. I said Dr. Milton was from Lower Durwood. That's where he has his surgery. The woman herself had been living at Marlby."

"Oh. And does she have a name?"

"Yes. She was a Miss Emily Fosdyke, a former almoner at this hospital."

"I see," said Spence thoughtfully. "So you knew her, then?"

"I did, yes."

Spence paused for a moment, apparently turning something over in his mind. "But they don't call them almoners any longer, do they?" he asked.

"No, they're known as medical social workers, and have been since about 1964. But they were called almoners when I was a lad, and they were certainly called almoners when Miss Fosdyke was appointed."

"And do they still do the same sort of work?"

"Yes. They're troubleshooters, really. They give advice and assistance to patients on a whole range of personal problems. The idea is that they work in conjunction with the medical staff to see that mental and emotional stresses don't get in the way of a proper recovery."

"I see," said Spence slowly. "So it's skilled work?"

"Oh yes. Good almoners are usually in short supply."

"And Miss Fosdyke was a good one?"

"Oh yes. Very efficient. Slightly stern and fierce, but very kind-hearted at bottom. She wouldn't stand any nonsense, didn't like slackers and malingerers, but if you had a genuine problem, she would put her back into helping you."

"And you say she was now retired?"

"Yes."

"When?"

"Oh, about three or four months ago."

"And she'd gone to live at Marlby?"

"Sort of. She took a job there, actually, living in as a kind of companion-cum-nurse to Lady Dinnister at Marlby Manor."

"Ah," said Spence. "Marlby Manor."

"You sound as if you know the place," said Dunbar.

"I do, yes. Lady Dinnister had some silver stolen a few years ago, and I went there a few times then."

"Oh, I see.' Dunbar absorbed this information and then proceeded. "Well, as I say, Emily Fosdyke was wheeled in here yesterday morning with a request for a postmortem, so naturally I did it myself."

"Naturally," said Spence dryly. "For old times' sake."

"Quite. Well, it wasn't quite as interesting a case as the last one we worked on together, but it did have its moments, nonetheless."

"And what did you find?"

"Well — it was quite intriguing, really. Emily Fosdyke always struck me as being a rather tough old bird when alive and kicking — she didn't look her age at all — so I was a bit surprised to find that she'd succumbed so soon after retiring. According to Dr. Milton, she was found dead in bed at Marlby Manor early yesterday morning, and the only clues were that she'd suffered very severe attacks of vomiting and diarrhea during the night."

"Did anyone attend to her during the night?"

"No. She had a private bathroom, and she seems to have staggered back and forth a few times, leaving traces in the toilet bowl and on the floor here and there."

"So she was pretty violently ill?"

"She certainly was. And normally, of course, one would assume that in a woman of sixty the vomiting and choking and whatnot had precipitated heart failure and thus death."

"But ... "

"Well," said Dunbar carefully, "we've analysed the contents of her stomach and her blood, and we've found extensive traces of arsenic in solution."

"Arsenic?" said Spence in surprise. "That's a bit old-fashioned, isn't it?"

Dunbar chuckled. "Old-fashioned it may be, my friend, but it's still very, very effective if you want to kill someone, believe you me. I've been doing some research on it, as a matter of fact. Do you want to hear about it?"

"Yes, please," said Spence.

Dunbar licked his right forefinger and turned over a page in the folder in front of him. "Right then. According to the sources of information immediately to hand, there are approximately five deaths per year in this country as a result of arsenic poisoning. Those are the ones we actually know about, of course. It's my guess that there are a good few others which aren't recognised. The main symptoms are severe and persistent gastroenteritis — "

"Which is what Miss Fosdyke had."

"Exactly. These symptoms begin within one hour of taking the arsenic, and death comes about in twenty-four to forty-eight hours. As you know, cases of gastroenteritis are fairly common, and only a minute percentage of them are caused by arsenic, which is why I suggest that there may well be cases of poisoning which go unnoticed. However, in this case we are told that Miss Fosdyke was perfectly okay the night before, which means that she died rather more quickly than usual. And from our point of view, it's just as well she did, because that meant that there were sizeable quantities of arsenic left in her blood. If she'd lasted for four days, the traces of arsenic would have disappeared entirely, and we would never have known about it. As for your point about it being an old-fashioned poison, well, it's perfectly true that before 1960 arsenic was rather more easily accessible than it is now and featured in some very famous cases."

"*Rex versus Madeleine Smith*, 1857," said Spence.

"Yes, and the case of Harold Greenwood, and others. Since 1960, however, arsenic has been rather harder to come by, at least in theory."

"But ... " said Spence again.

"Yes, but it is indeed," said Dunbar, raising his eyebrows and turning over another sheet of paper. "I must say I was rather taken aback by what my authorities tell me. One writer, Curry, says that in a murder case that he was involved in, it was found that literally tons of arsenic were available quite close to the scene of the murder, in a glassworks."

Spence swore under his breath. "Charming," he said. "But you seem to be quite convinced that Miss Fosdyke was murdered — and there must be at least a possibility that it was suicide, surely?"

"Yes," said Dunbar, nodding gravely. "Yes, I have to admit that there is that possibility."

"And we're back to the 'buts' again, are we?"

"Yes, we certainly are. If I were a retired hospital almoner with a fair working knowledge of death and drugs in various forms, I doubt very much if I would kill myself by dissolving a stiff dose of arsenic in water, or whatever, and drinking it."

"But it is possible."

"Oh, it's possible, yes. Anything in this life is possible. But I knew Miss Fosdyke personally, over a great many years, and I am here to tell you that she was not the suicidal type. Far from it."

"But the people who saw a lot of her over the last few months, since she retired, they may have a different view?"

"They may, yes, and you'll have to ask them, of course. But for starters I can tell you that Lady Dinnister herself suggested to Dr. Milton that the cause of death needed very careful investigation."

"Oh? Why did she do that?"

"I don't know. You'll have to ask her. And if you do come to the conclusion that it was murder, just remember that arsenic is not very difficult to get hold of and administer. Anyone with access to a reasonable public library could do what I did — read up on it in half an hour and find out the details of the law governing its sale, likely commercial sources, and how to dissolve it."

"How much arsenic do you need to kill someone?"

"Oh, two grains. Say a small pinch of it."

"It's a powder, is it?"

"Yes. It's white, usually. And in this case, as I've said, it was mixed with a fluid. In that form it's odorless and tasteless, apart from a slight aftertaste."

"Could the aftertaste be masked by another flavour?"

"Yes, so I understand, quite easily. One of its chief uses is as a weedkiller and, according to one book I read, over eight hundred million pounds of it are used annually in the U.S.A. alone. That's enough to kill every man, woman, and child in America many times over. And, for that matter, the wind and the rain have been known to blow it off the land onto food being prepared in kitchens."

"Can you actually go out and buy it in this country?" asked Inspector Laurel.

"Technically, no," said Dunbar. "That is to say, you couldn't buy it yourself. It's illegal to sell it, except to a doctor, a vet, or a research institute. But it can be sold wholesale for sheep dip, provided it's clearly labelled with a warning. And it's also sold wholesale, as I've said, as a weedkiller."

"And bought, presumably, by local authorities and schools and so on," Laurel continued.

"Yes. I gather that in that form it often has a dye mixed into it, in the hope of providing an additional warning if anyone mixes it into your drink."

Laurel added to the notes that he had been making throughout the discussion.

Spence folded his hands in front of him. "Well, is that the lot, then?"

"It's all I can do for you at the moment, Ben. I'll send you the paperwork when it's all typed up. The only other thing I can do is to wish you the very best of luck." He grinned.

"Thanks very much," said Spence without smiling back. "It looks as if I shall need it."

Ten

Before leaving the hospital, Spence followed his invariable practice in a murder case and visited the mortuary to view Miss Fosdyke's body. Then he returned to Dr. Dunbar's office and telephoned Marlby Manor.

His call was answered by Mr. Tanner in the best traditions of butlerage. Spence explained who he was and asked if it would be convenient if he could call on Lady Dinnister in about half an hour's time. There was a short pause while Tanner buzzed Lady Dinnister to find out the answer, which was affirmative, and then the two police officers left Dr. Dunbar and went outside to Spence's car.

Spence was driving a Ford Granada 2.3 Ghia these days, and he slid behind the wheel and guided it briskly out of the hospital carpark. A few minutes later he and Laurel were on the main road to the southwest out of Wellbridge, heading towards Marlby.

"What do you know about Lady Dinnister?" asked Spence.

"Not much," said Laurel. "I've heard of her, but that's about all. She's fairly elderly, isn't she?"

"Yes, I imagine she's into her seventies by now. Leading a fairly quiet life these days, I gather, but in the old days she was quite a goer."

"Oh — in what way?"

"Oh, social life, charity work, local politics. Back in the thirties, Marlby Manor was one of the famous country houses: lots of guests down from London every weekend, big parties, the occasional ball. All highly respectable but very cheerful and light-hearted."

Laurel grunted. "Hm. The war put an end to all that, I suppose."

"Yes. That and a lot of other things."

"Was there a Lord Dinnister?"

"Not Lord Dinnister, no. A Sir Somebody Dinnister, but I can't remember the name. Anyway, he was a businessman, something in the city with a lot of money behind him. Later on he was an M.P."

"Conservative?"

Spence laughed. "Naturally."

"Was Marlby Manor his family home?"

"Yes, I suppose it must have been. It wasn't Lady Dinnister's, that's for sure. Her family came from the Downsea area. Her father was an army man and a gentleman farmer, lord lieutenant of the county."

"You said you'd had some dealings with them before," said Laurel.

Spence overtook an exceptionally long lorry before answering. "Yes. About ten years ago, just before Lady Dinnister's husband died. They had some silver stolen, and I was in charge of finding it. Fortunately I got lucky, and the pots were back on their sideboard within twenty-four hours, so that did my career no harm."

Laurel laughed. "No," he said, "I can imagine."

"Let's hope we have the same sort of luck this time."

Ten minutes later Spence turned his car in through the east gate of Marlby Manor and drove steadily up the tarmac drive to the house. To the left of the drive was a large, open expanse of grass, which had not been improved by the lack of rain and the persistent sunshine over the past two weeks. To the right, over a high brick wall, lay the kitchen garden. Occasionally, behind the house, it was just possible to catch a glimpse of the lake and the wood beyond it.

Spence brought his car to a halt at the front of the house, where the drive broadened out to provide sufficient parking space for a whole convoy of visitors. In fact, only one other car was there at present: Lady Dinnister's impressive Rolls-Royce. Len Jones was doing what he always did when there was nothing more urgent to do — namely, polishing its bodywork until the reflected light became positively blinding.

Spence eyed Jones with the habitual care of an experienced detective. What he saw was a man of just under thirty, perhaps six-feet-two-inches tall, with broad, muscular shoulders. Despite his size, Jones moved easily, in a very relaxed, flowing manner, like an athlete or a well-trained boxer. He was wearing medium-grey trousers, a white shirt, and an old tie; the matching jacket and a chauffeur's cap were laid neatly on the grass nearby. Spence noted that the chauffeur looked at the visitors carefully, assessing them shrewdly but not allowing his gaze to appear rude.

Spence nodded at him. "Good morning."

"Good morning, sir," said Jones in return, and went on with his polishing.

Spence approached the heavy wooden front door and rang the bell. The door was opened almost immediately by Tanner, who, despite the August heat, was wearing a black jacket, a waistcoat, grey-striped trousers and black shoes. His collar appeared rather too tight, and his neck bulged out above it; the bulge was echoed lower down by his extensive waistline. Tanner was largely bald, with a round brown dome to his head and a brown face; what hair he had left was black, lightly oiled, and brushed in a band around the back of his head. He looked every inch the dignified butler and only just avoided pomposity.

"Detective Chief Superintendent Spence?" Tanner asked as he opened the door.

"And Detective Inspector Laurel," said Spence.

"Please come in, gentlemen. Lady Dinnister asked me to show you upstairs at once."

"Thank you."

Spence and Laurel stepped inside and then followed the butler up the broad staircase to Lady Dinnister's sitting room.

Tanner announced them and ushered them inside before discreetly disappearing.

Lady Dinnister was with her secretary, dictating letters. She greeted Spence with obvious pleasure and recognition.

"Ah, Mr. Spence," she said. "How very nice to see you again." She held out her hand, and Spence crossed the room to greet her. "You must excuse me not getting up, but legs are not what they were."

"Please don't apologise," said Spence. "I quite understand."

Spence then introduced his colleague, and Lady Dinnister introduced Susan Green, who blushed nervously and looked down at the pad on her knee, fingering the spiral wire backing as if to make sure it was still there. Spence did not want to embarrass the girl further and simply smiled at her before returning his attention to the old lady.

"Now sit down, sit down," said Lady Dinnister. "Make yourselves at home."

Spence and Laurel drew up two chairs to enable them to converse comfortably, and they had no sooner sat down than the door opened again and Hazel Quinn appeared, carrying a large silver tray.

"Ah, good," said Lady Dinnister. "I asked to have some coffee brought up as soon as you arrived. Let's have it over here, Hazel."

Hazel deposited the tray on a small table in the centre of the group and poured out four cups of coffee with or without cream, as requested. As she did so, Spence ran his eyes over her, which was a far from painful experience. Despite the butcher's apron she was wearing, a large area of cleavage was revealed through the V-neck of Hazel's blouse as she bent forward to pour the coffee. It was with some reluctance that Spence finally lowered his gaze to the coffeepot.

"I see you're still putting your silver to its proper use," he remarked.

Lady Dinnister smiled. "I was wondering if you would remember."

"Oh yes, I remember very well."

"I was very pleased to hear your name when you phoned this morning. It gave me some confidence in the outcome of our discussions."

"I'm glad to hear it," said Spence.

Hazel departed, and for a few minutes the four of them discussed silver, its rising cost, the problems of keeping it secure, and the pleasures of good design.

"Miss Fosdyke used to say that this coffeepot really belonged in a museum," Lady Dinnister remarked eventually.

"Which would be a waste, in my view," said Spence. "I'd rather see it here, in active use." He put down his empty cup. "But it is, of course, about Miss Fosdyke that we've come to see you."

Lady Dinnister's eyes momentarily flickered shut, as if she felt a spasm of pain. She leaned back in her chair. "Ah yes, of course. Poor Emily Fosdyke ... You've had the result of the postmortem, I suppose?"

"Yes."

"Would it be unethical to ask what killed her?"

Spence paused. "I'm tempted to say heart failure."

Lady Dinnister smiled. "We all die of that. But what caused the heart to fail?"

"It was a poison," said Spence after a moment. "Arsenic."

Susan Green gasped, and raised the back of her hand to her mouth. Her eyes were almost comically wide and shocked. Everyone turned to look at her, but she didn't blush this time; she went white instead.

Lady Dinnister merely sighed. "Arsenic," she said sadly.

"You don't seem very surprised."

"No. I'm not surprised, not really. I suppose there's no chance whatever that it might have been natural causes?"

60

"Not in the sense you mean, no. There's a remote chance that the poison was ingested accidentally, but only a remote one. Did Miss Fosdyke eat the same meals as yourself in the twenty-four hours before she died?"

"I've thought about that very carefully," said Lady Dinnister. "And the answer is that we ate the same meals for at least the previous forty-eight hours, with the possible exception of tomato sauce, or salt and pepper."

"Well, in that case," said Spence, "the chances of the arsenic being taken accidentally are very slim indeed."

"I see," said Lady Dinnister slowly. "So you think it was deliberate. Which means that she either took it herself, or someone gave it to her?"

"Yes."

Lady Dinnister's expression remained unchanged, but Susan Green suddenly let out a series of small sobs, as if hardly able to believe her ears. No one took any notice of her, as that seemed to be the kindest way to respond.

"I see," said Lady Dinnister again. Her eyes were focused on a far corner of the room, her mind sorting out the various implications of what she had been told. "So, let us consider the first of those possibilities: the idea that she took the poison herself."

"Yes," Spence agreed, "let's consider the question of suicide. Had Miss Fosdyke been at all depressed recently?"

Lady Dinnister gave a grim chuckle. "If you had known Miss Fosdyke," she said, "you would have known that she was not the type of woman who would have allowed herself to suffer depression. She was a very strong character indeed. Too strong for comfort at times."

"What do you think, Miss Green?" asked Spence, turning to the secretary. "Do you think Miss Fosdyke had been depressed?"

Susan Green visibly pulled herself together; she lowered her chin and swallowed hard. "No. No, I agree with Lady Dinnister. Miss Fosdyke didn't seem depressed to me — not at all."

"Did she ever discuss with either of you the possibility of killing herself?"

"No, never," said Miss Green positively.

Lady Dinnister shook her head.

"And on Monday she seemed her normal, cheerful self?"

"Well, normal, certainly," said Lady Dinnister. "She was, as I've said, an eminently well-balanced person in every respect. Surprisingly so, considering she was a spinster."

"Fair enough," said Spence. "So for the moment we'll rule out suicide. Tell me what happened on Monday. What did you do all day?"

Lady Dinnister folded her hands in her lap and cast her mind back. "Well, Miss Fosdyke lived in, of course, as you know. And it was an ordinary sort of day. We got up, had breakfast, and then I attended to some business in the morning. In the afternoon we went for a drive."

"In the Rolls?"

"Yes."

"And your chauffeur was driving?"

"Yes."

"Where did you go?"

"We went down to Lime Beach. Miss Fosdyke has had a bungalow there for some years. She bought it when house prices started to go mad, otherwise she would never have been able to afford anything when she retired."

"And she rented it out, I suppose."

"Yes, usually. Sometimes to holiday-makers, sometimes to students. It's empty at the moment, and has been for some weeks, so the main purpose of our visit was to make sure that the house was still in one piece. No vandalism or anything."

"And how did you find it?"

"Oh, it was all in good order."

"What time did you get back?"

"About … five o'clock."

"Then what?"

"Well, nothing much. I watched some cricket on television, and then we had dinner. After dinner we read for a bit, and then about ten o'clock I went to bed. Miss Fosdyke helped me, of course."

"Was that usual?"

"Oh yes. That was why she was here, really, She wasn't a nurse exactly, though I'm sure she knew more about medicine than most nurses, and she was very good at just giving me that little bit of assistance that I need. She was also a great deal more intelligent and interesting to talk to than most hired help."

Lady Dinnister paused. For the first time, emotion seemed likely to take over; her lower lip trembled for a second and was then firmly controlled. She drew a deep breath and managed to continue.

"I was very fond of Miss Fosdyke, in my way. I shall certainly miss her very much."

Spence carried on with his questioning. "And after Miss Fosdyke helped you to bed, she presumably went to bed herself?"

"I've no reason to suppose otherwise."

Spence nodded. "What did you have to eat that day?"

"Well, we both had the same meals, as I've said. For lunch we had cold beef, followed by cheese and biscuits. In the evening we both had a tomato juice, followed by trout with almonds and fruit salad."

"You both drank coffee?"

"Yes."

"From the same pot?"

"Yes."

"What about a nightcap?"

"Ah. Now I had cocoa at about ten o'clock."

"And Miss Fosdyke didn't?"

"Not at that stage, no. Sometimes she joined me, sometimes she didn't. On Monday night she said she didn't fancy it."

"Was that because she wasn't feeling well?"

"No, not as far as I know. She made no complaint, and she looked all right. Quite hale and hearty, in fact."

"All right," said Spence. "Let's move on to yesterday morning. Who first discovered that Miss Fosdyke was dead?"

"My housekeeper, Hazel Quinn."

"She was the one who served us coffee?"

"Yes."

"And what did she do when she first found Miss Fosdyke?"

"Well, as far as I know, she went downstairs and told Tanner, my butler. She got him to ring for the doctor, and then she came upstairs and told me."

"Did she see a note left by the bedside?"

"Well, she certainly never mentioned it if she did."

"And you think she would have done?"

"Oh yes. Hazel is a most steady and sensible woman. I value her services highly."

"What did you do when you were told about the situation?"

"Well, I got up, with some difficulty, and went and had a look for myself."

"Did you notice anything unusual in the room?"

"Not unusual, no," said Lady Dinnister carefully. "However, there was one thing there that was quite normal and expected, but which I felt was of some importance."

"And what was that?"

"It was an empty glass by the bedside."

"Ah," said Spence, "now we're getting somewhere. So Miss Fosdyke did have a nightcap after all?"

"Yes," said Lady Dinnister. "Perhaps I should have mentioned that earlier when we were talking about the cocoa. You see, it was no secret — and Emily often mentioned it when she was doing the cocoa for me — that she herself usually preferred something alcoholic at bedtime. Not every night, but probably four times out of five."

"Any particular tipple?"

"No, so long as it was fairly strong. Sherry, Madeira, whisky, that sort of thing. It was to put her to sleep, you see; that was the point. She said it was far better than sleeping pills, and much safer. But apart from a glass at night, she wasn't much of a drinker — almost teetotal in fact."

"Oh," Spence grunted. "And I suppose this glass that you noticed was washed up and put away, was it?"

"No," said Lady Dinnister firmly. "It was not. I kept it."

Spence glanced at Laurel and grinned. He was amused by the old lady's crisp response, and also delighted that with any luck he would be able to check whether Miss Fosdyke's nightcap had caused her death.

Somewhat unsteadily, Lady Dinnister began to rise to her feet. Miss Green quickly crossed to the old lady's side and supported her.

With a muttered complaint about the stiffness of her joints, Lady Dinnister walked to a cupboard beside the window and returned with a wineglass held by the stem. She handed it to Spence, who by now was also on his feet.

"Here you are, my friend," she said. "It's all yours. That's a clue."

"It is indeed," said Spence. "Probably a very important one."

"And as you can see, there is still a trace of sherry in the bottom."

Spence sniffed at the glass carefully. "Yes, I believe you're right."

"Of course I'm right," said Lady Dinnister testily. "At the age of seventy-two, I know sherry when I smell it, and in any case the bottle's in Fosdyke's room."

The old lady sat down again, and Spence winked at Laurel.

"Well, that's extremely useful," he said. "But what made you think it was worth preserving unwashed?"

Lady Dinnister looked up at him. "Well, Mr. Spence, I may as well admit it. Fundamentally, I'm a very nervous and selfish and apprehensive old woman. If I hadn't been frightened of looking foolish, I would have contacted the police myself over the weekend. You see, for some days before Miss Fosdyke died, I had had the very clear impression that someone was trying to kill me."

"To kill you?"

"Yes."

Spence and Laurel exchanged a glance. "What gave you that idea?"

"There were three things really, but whether you will regard them as adequate grounds for suspicion, I don't know." Lady Dinnister counted off the items on her fingers. "First of all, a week ago last Monday, I was sent a bouquet of flowers. The flowers had a piece of sharp, dirty wire wrapped around them. It pierced my hand, and I had to have an antitetanus injection. At the time I thought that the incident was very odd, and if someone had poisoned that spike of wire, I might well be dead myself. Number two: on Thursday of last week, a wheel came loose on my Rolls-Royce, and we nearly had a serious accident. I was quite badly shaken up and banged my face as the car lurched off the road. Admittedly, the car had been serviced the previous day, and the wheel might not have been tightened up properly, but the garage owner was adamant that it was perfectly all right when it left him. And number three: last Friday night poor Hazel was nearly electrocuted by my hair-dryer. When that happened, I took the wretched thing to pieces myself. And you can call me hysterical if you like, but it looked very much to me as if someone had scraped the covering off that wire deliberately."

"Causing a shock through the outer case?" said Spence.

"Yes."

"I see." Spence was serious. "Well, I'll certainly look into those incidents, and I'm glad you told me about them. You obviously don't feel that they were accidents."

"No," said Lady Dinnister firmly. "I do not. So you see, Mr. Spence, I was half-expecting something awful to happen, and now it has. Not to me, but to poor Emily Fosdyke."

Lady Dinnister looked up at Spence, her eyes brimming with tears.

"It may seem silly," she said, "and perhaps I'm getting a bit old and foolish, but I must ask you to consider the possibility that the poison which killed Miss Fosdyke was really intended for me."

Eleven

Mr. Tanner unlocked Miss Fosdyke's bedroom door.

"Lady Dinnister wanted it kept locked," he told Spence and Laurel, "so naturally we did as she asked."

The butler swung the door open but made no attempt to enter. Spence stepped through the entrance and examined the lock on the solid, sturdy door.

"Who has a key to this room?" he asked.

"Lady Dinnister and myself."

"Did Miss Fosdyke have one?"

"No sir, I don't believe she did. There was no need for it when she was alive."

"I see." Spence glanced at the butler, who moved nervously, folding his hands behind him and jangling the keys when he realised that Spence's eyes were on him.

"Where do you keep your keys, Mr. Tanner?"

"Well, I … usually carry them on me."

"You have keys to all the rooms in the house?"

"Yes sir."

"And what do you do with them when you go to bed?" The butler again shifted his position uncertainly. He tugged at his left earlobe and looked at Laurel, despite the fact that he was answering Spence's question. "Well sir, I, er, I keep them on my dressing table."

"Yes, I see. So Miss Fosdyke did not usually keep her bedroom door locked, but it has been locked since her body was removed?"

"Yes sir, once we'd cleaned up. As I say, Lady Dinnister thought it was best."

"Quite," said Spence. "Right you are, Mr. Tanner, thank you for opening up." Spence glanced inside the room and then looked back at the butler. "I shan't need to keep you, but would you be kind enough to ask the housekeeper to come up?"

"Of course, sir," said Tanner, and with a slight bow he turned and went off down the stairs, his dignity and calm demeanor apparently fully restored.

Spence watched him go for a moment and then returned his attention to the room. "Now then," he said, "let's see what we've got here."

The two detectives went inside the late Miss Fosdyke's bedroom and began to look around. It was not an exercise which took very long.

The bedroom was large by most standards, with two windows that faced north. Leading off the bedroom, to the right of one of the windows, was a bathroom. The bedroom was fully carpeted, and the curtains were of red velvet; all other furnishings were of similarly high quality. There was a single bed with a headboard, bedside tables on each side of it, and a reading light above it. Under the window on the left was a small bureau with a chair; the lid of the bureau was shut but not locked, and when it was opened, a large number of old letters and several pads of notepaper were revealed. Miss Fosdyke had evidently been an assiduous correspondent. Beside the other window was an easy chair, with a small table nearby, on which lay a pile of women's magazines. Along the wall immediately to the right of the door was a spacious built-in wardrobe with cupboards rising to ceiling height above it. To the left of the wardrobe was a dressing table, with Miss Fosdyke's hair brush and various small pieces of jewelry arranged neatly on a glass tray.

Briefly, without conducting a complete search at this stage, the two men poked around, opening drawers, glancing at the addresses on the letters, examining the clothes hanging in the wardrobe. The aim was simply to get the feel of the situation, to try to form a preliminary judgement as to what sort of person Miss Fosdyke had been.

"Well," said Laurel after a few minutes, "it's all beautifully arranged. Either Miss Fosdyke was pathologically neat and tidy, or else this room has just been given the most thorough cleaning it's had in years."

Spence sighed. "Yes," he said, "I'm inclined to agree with you."

Spence made a brief excursion into the bathroom, where he found everything even more conspicuously hygienic than in the bedroom. Then he came back to join Laurel. As he did so, there was a knock on the bedroom door.

"Just a moment," called Spence. "I expect that'll be the housekeeper," he told Laurel in a quiet tone. "But before I let her in, I want to make one point to you. It's an important point, and it's as well that we should both bear it in mind because you and I are inevitably going to be viewing the evidence from slightly different angles. Now, the point is this. In any murder enquiry it's vital to establish what happened. But what seems to have happened at first sight is not always what will be seen to have happened later on when we know more. In other words, what we've got to bear in mind is that there may well be other possible explanations of the facts besides the apparent or obvious one. Do you follow me?"

"Yes," said Laurel after a moment, "I do. It sounds a bit metaphysical, but I think I get the drift of it."

"Good," said Spence. "What I really mean is that as we go along, and as we learn more and more, we've got to be continuously reviewing all our previous assessments in the light of new evidence ... Now, let's see that housekeeper."

Laurel crossed to the door and opened it to reveal Hazel Quinn, standing with her hands linked in front of her. "Sorry to have kept you," he said. "Please come inside."

"Thank you," said Hazel, and did as she was asked.

"Come and sit down. Miss Quinn," said Spence, motioning Hazel towards the easy chair. "It is 'Miss,' isn't it?"

"Yes," said Hazel. "I was married once, but I'm not now. Would you like me to sit here?"

"Yes please. I'd like to have a little chat, and you might as well be comfortable."

Hazel settled herself in the chair by the window; she seemed slightly surprised to be asked to take a seat, but not at all apprehensive. Spence perched on the end of the bed, and Laurel sat on the chair by the bureau.

Spence began by explaining who he was and why he and Laurel were at the manor. As he did so, he made a careful note of Hazel's appearance; he particularly noticed her full figure, the eyes that, despite the thick glasses, were clearly crossed, and the sensible working shoes with firm, solid heels.

"Miss Quinn," he said, "I had the feeling when I saw you pouring the coffee that I'd seen you before somewhere. And it wasn't when I last came here some ten years ago."

"No," said Hazel, "I've only been here four years."

"No," said Spence thoughtfully. "So it must have been somewhere else. And my guess is that it was on the front of a calendar."

Hazel laughed aloud, her wide smile revealing white, even teeth.

"You're laughing," said Spence, "but does that mean I'm right or wrong?"

"Oh, you're quite right," said Hazel. "Quite right."

"It was the glasses that threw me for a while — you didn't wear them as a model."

"No." Hazel reached up. She took off her glasses and half-closed her eyes, turning her head so that the north light lit up her features to best advantage. "There ... does that bring it back?"

"Ah yes," said Spence. "That and the figure, of course. You still keep in pretty good shape, I see."

Hazel put her glasses back on. "Oh yes, I'm not over the hill yet."

"But it must be — oh — twenty years since your pictures first began to appear?"

"More than that," said Hazel. "I was fourteen when I first started."

"And how did that come about?"

Hazel gave him a straight look. Many men would not have received an answer to that question, and it was evident from her manner that she did not feel intimidated in the presence of two police officers. But there had been something about the friendly tone of voice in which the question had been asked that made it acceptable to her.

"Well," she said, "it's all a long time ago now, but I was living at home in those days. My father was a smallholder. He kept a few pigs and scratched a living off a few acres of land. Anyway, one day a photographer came along and offered Dad a fiver if he would let him use the barn to pose one of his models for a nudist magazine."

"Which magazine was that?" asked Spence. "Good old *Health and Efficiency*, I suppose?"

"Either that or *The Naturist*," said Hazel, "I can't remember which. Anyway, the fiver was big money for my dad, and when the photographer offered another fiver for my services. Dad couldn't get my clothes off quick enough."

Spence chuckled with amusement at the thought. "And how many of you were there in the family?"

"Oh, three boys and three girls, all told."

"Do you still keep in touch with them?"

"Oh yes."

"And I suppose after those first pictures of you appeared, you went from strength to strength?"

"Yes, I was in great demand, even if I do say so myself."

"And I seem to remember you were in occasional films, too."

"Oh, only bit parts," said Hazel modestly. "They didn't pay very much."

"But you did make a living as a model?"

"Yes. As a model and a stripper. The sixties were good years for strippers. Until the government made it illegal to have gambling and cabaret in the same club."

"Ah yes," said Spence, "that did make a difference. And then at some stage I imagine you got tired of living out of a suitcase?"

Hazel sighed. "Yes. It was only fun for so long, and then I got the urge to settle down. I still do the odd stag night, even today. I did one for the police not so long ago. But I'd always been interested in cookery, so I decided to take that up instead. You can go on doing that until they plant you."

"Yes indeed," said Spence. "But let's go back a bit. I think you said you were married at one stage."

"For a while, yes."

"What happened?"

Hazel lifted her chin and looked at Spence directly. This was another question which might often have received a rude answer. "He drank, Superintendent. At first I thought I could cure him, of course. Women always do. But I couldn't. He always went back to the bottle, and when I found that out, I left him."

Spence nodded and paused for a second. "Well, Hazel, that's all very interesting, but not perhaps immediately relevant. What I really want to ask you about is Miss Fosdyke."

"Yes." Hazel glanced down at her hands. "It's a sad business."

"And I believe you were the one who found her?"

"Yes, that's right. When I brought her a cup of tea."

"Did you do that every morning?"

"Yes."

"Show me what happened when you came in."

"You mean, walk through it?"

"Yes."

71

"Okay."

Hazel rose to her feet and crossed to the door. Then, without any self-consciousness, she mimed her actions of the previous day. She came into the room and put down her invisible tray on the bedside table.

"I looked at her as I did this," said Hazel, "and I could see her eyes were open. Her mouth, too. I got a bit scared then. Anyway, I went to the window" — Hazel moved — "drew open the curtains" — she swept her hands apart — "and looked back. Till I was sure ... Then I went downstairs."

Spence nodded. "Fair enough. Did you notice anything unusual?"

"Only the smell." Hazel sniffed. "It still pongs a bit, even now."

"Who cleaned the room?"

"I did."

"You vacuumed, dusted, washed the sheets, I suppose?"

"Yes, all that. Gave it a real thorough clean, here and in the bathroom." Hazel paused as a thought struck her. "Oh. Perhaps that wasn't such a good idea?"

Spence shrugged. "It can't be helped. Did you empty the vacuum cleaner?"

"Yes."

"And have the dustbin men come?"

"Yes. Half past eight this morning."

"Hmm. Did you take anything out of the room, other than the sheets and dust?"

"No."

"And you left all Miss Fosdyke's clothes and possessions?"

"Yes. I didn't go in the drawers much. Lady Dinnister got in touch with Miss Fosdyke's sister, up north somewhere — I believe she's coming down on Friday to sort things out."

Spence nodded. "All right. Now where did Miss Fosdyke keep her sherry?"

"Sherry?" Hazel seemed puzzled.

"Yes. I gather she liked a nightcap."

"Well — over there, I suppose." Hazel rose and went to one of the cupboards above the built-in wardrobe. She swung open the door at head height and looked inside. "Yes. Here it is."

Spence came across the room to join her in looking at the bottle of sherry, which was the only visible object in what appeared to be an otherwise empty cupboard. "How did you know it was there?"

Hazel shrugged. "Well, I don't know. I suppose I must have seen it when I was cleaning."

"Did Miss Fosdyke ever offer you a drink?"

"Not in here she didn't, no. But as you say, this was for nightcaps, and there's plenty of sherry elsewhere in the house."

"Was Miss Fosdyke friendly toward you?"

"Oh yes. She was friendly, but we weren't friends, if you know what I mean."

"Yes," said Spence, "I know exactly what you mean. Did she ever talk of killing herself?"

"Good God, no."

"If Miss Fosdyke had been taken ill in the night, would you have expected her to call for help?"

Hazel pondered for a moment. "Well, no, I don't think she would. She wouldn't have wanted to be a nuisance. She'd have just gone into the bathroom to be sick and then crawled back into bed."

"Yes, that's what I thought. Did Miss Fosdyke have any enemies?"

Hazel glanced at Spence, and then at Laurel; her face went a little pale as she absorbed the drift of Spence's thinking. "Certainly not — not in the way you mean."

"What way do I mean?"

"Well — none of us disliked her enough to wish her any harm. None of us was great friends with her — but she'd only been here three months, and she kept her distance."

"I see." Spence looked at the wall to the left of the door. "What do we have next-door?"

"It's a storeroom."

"And where's the nearest other bedroom that's slept in?"

"Oh, that's Lady Dinnister's. Deliberately so."

"In case Lady Dinnister needed any help in the night, I suppose?"

"Yes." Hazel smiled rather sadly. "Funny that, isn't it?"

*

After a few more questions, Hazel was dismissed, and Spence and Laurel concentrated their attention on the bottle of sherry. Spence lifted it carefully out of the cupboard and slipped it into a polyethylene bag that Laurel had fetched from their car. Then Spence held it up against the light.

"About one glass taken out of it, I should say. Well, that should make things a little easier. I want the bottle fingerprinted and the contents analysed. If someone did mix arsenic with her sherry, we should soon know."

"They could hardly have mixed it in the glass," said Laurel. "Not once she'd poured it out, not without her knowing."

"Exactly."

"Our friend Hazel didn't seem very surprised at the idea that Miss Fosdyke might have been murdered." Laurel remarked.

"No, well, I expect the fact that we're thinking in terms of murder is beginning to penetrate through the household. And once it starts, it'll take all of three minutes before everyone knows."

While Laurel was tying a label on the polyethylene bag, Spence stood up on tiptoe to check that there was nothing else in the cupboard where they had found the sherry. But, in fact, there was something else: a small piece of card, so thin and so flat on the shelf that it might easily have been overlooked. Spence flicked it forward with a fingernail and then picked it up with a pair of tweezers.

"Well now, what's this?" He held up the card and read aloud. "Williams and Williams, Wine Merchants, High Street, Wellbridge. I quote: 'To Lady Dinnister. Please accept this bottle of fine amontillado sherry with our compliments.'"

"Is it handwritten?" asked Laurel, looking up from his work on the bag.

"No — typed. Ten characters to the inch, I should say."

"Oh. Well, handwritten or not, the implication is the same either way. If Miss Fosdyke was poisoned by this bottle of sherry, then Lady Dinnister was right. Someone *was* trying to kill her, and Miss Fosdyke got it by mistake."

"Yes," said Spence slowly. "Yes. It does look that way, doesn't it?"

Twelve

Detective Inspector Laurel went downstairs to put the bottle of sherry in the car while Spence returned to Lady Dinnister's sitting room.

"What, more questions?" asked Lady Dinnister as he entered the room.

Spence smiled. "Yes, I'm afraid so. And there are going to be a lot more over the next few days."

Susan Green, who was evidently still taking dictation, hurriedly pulled off her glasses and began to collect up her papers and pens. "Would you like me to go?" she asked hesitantly.

"No, no, please stay for the moment," said Spence.

Lady Dinnister motioned him to a chair, and he sat down.

"Well now," he continued, "for the moment I'm working on the hypothesis that Miss Fosdyke died as a result of ingesting arsenic that had been mixed with sherry. That seems to be the most likely explanation. We've found a bottle of sherry in her room, and we'll send it away to be analysed. But we've also found, in the same cupboard as the sherry, a small card."

Spence took the wine merchants' card, now safely covered in clear polyethylene, out of his pocket and held it up.

"It's a printed card that carries the name of Williams and Williams, Wine Merchants, of the High Street, Wellbridge. Have you ever done any business with them?"

"No," said Lady Dinnister. "Not as far as I remember."

"Oh. Well, that might account for the card. Anyway, it says on it, 'To Lady Dinnister. Please accept this bottle of fine amontillado sherry with our compliments.'"

"Does it indeed?"

"Yes. Now — did you receive this bottle of sherry and give it to Miss Fosdyke to try out?"

"No."

"So if it was sent here by Williams and Williams, she took it without your knowledge?"

"Yes."

"Was that in character?"

Lady Dinnister made a doubtful face. "Well, yes and no. Emily was not, of course, a thief. If she'd wanted a glass of sherry, or even a whole crateful, she could have had it. There's plenty of sherry and wine in the cellar, and within reason she could have helped herself. And, of course, we do get a certain number of free samples — unsolicited gifts, that kind of thing."

"I see. So it's possible that the sherry was delivered here, and that Miss Fosdyke, short of a nightcap, took it up to her room."

"It's possible, yes. But I should have thought it very unlikely that she would do such a thing without telling me."

"Nevertheless, that does leave us with the possibility that she may have ended up drinking something that was really intended for you."

"Yes." Lady Dinnister's eyes became misty, and her lip trembled for a moment. "Dear me, what a dreadful thought. Perhaps someone really does hate me. Someone really does want me dead."

The old lady groped for her handkerchief and briefly dabbed at her eyes.

"If it's any comfort," said Spence, "I'm quite sure they won't be foolish enough to try it again. Not now the police are involved." Then he paused to give Lady Dinnister a moment or two to recover.

Susan Green's face, meanwhile, had assumed the horrified expression which it had borne almost throughout Spence s previous interview with her employer. She turned to look at Spence, clearly unable to understand the implications of what she was hearing.

"But, Superintendent, why on earth should anyone at Williams and Williams want to murder Lady Dinnister? We don't know anyone there; we've never had any dealings with them."

"I don't think it was anyone at Williams and Williams" said Spence kindly. "If what we're thinking turns out to be true, then I imagine someone stole that card and used it to introduce the sherry into the house in a way that would not arouse suspicion."

Susan's face registered her newfound comprehension; she nodded and then immediately blushed furiously. "Oh yes, of course," she said. "How stupid of me not to realise."

"Not at all," said Spence, smiling in an attempt to reassure her. "It's not everyone who thinks like a policeman."

Spence glanced back at Lady Dinnister. She had now controlled her momentary emotion, so he carried on with his questions.

"Did Miss Fosdyke normally keep her bedroom door locked?"

"Oh no. Not normally. In fact, I doubt if she had a key. We all trust each other — or we did."

"But you locked the room yesterday morning."

Lady Dinnister sighed heavily. "Yes, once poor Emily had been removed, we did, yes. It seemed the best thing to do, somehow."

"And who holds keys to that room?"

"I have a set, and Mr. Tanner has one, too."

At that point Laurel returned from the car. With a nod at Spence to indicate that all was well, he sat down slightly behind Spence, where he could take occasional notes unobtrusively. Spence felt that this was a good moment to ask Susan Green to leave, which she did with evident relief.

"I'd like to ask you some fairly frank questions," Spence told Lady Dinnister, "and I think you'll be able to speak more freely without your secretary present."

Lady Dinnister inclined her head in agreement. "Of course."

"Now, to get back to Mr. Tanner, your butler — how long has he been working for you?"

"Oh, about seven years."

"Do you trust him?"

"Certainly. I wouldn't have kept him if I didn't. He came with very good references, and it was only because his previous employer went abroad that he was looking for a job at all."

"I see. Well now, if we assume for the time being that it was the sherry that was poisoned, and that it was intended for you, we must consider the question of motive. And this is where things can get decidedly sticky."

"In what sense?"

"Well, what I'm asking you to do is to tell me a number of rather difficult things. One, is there anyone who hates you enough to want to kill you? Two, is there anyone who, while not apparently hating you, has a definite motive to kill you — in other words, who benefits from your death? And three, who do you know in either of those categories who has the necessary ruthlessness to actually go about killing you in a thoroughly cold-blooded manner? Because, believe me, if I'm right about the sherry, this was not an impulsive and hotheaded crime. This was a planned, considered, and deliberate decision to end the life of another human being."

Lady Dinnister was silent for some time, only the restless movement of her hands in her lap revealing the turmoil in her mind.

"Well," she said at last, "let's adopt a simplistic approach to begin with. First of all, nobody hates me, so far as I'm aware. I'm not conscious of ever having done anyone any great harm, either deliberately or accidentally."

"There've been no children killed by your car, no faithful retainers sacked at a moment's notice?"

"No. Oh, I've sacked people, of course — but treated them rather better than they deserved, I believe."

Spence nodded. "Right. So let's move on to number two. Who benefits from your death?"

"Well, I suppose what that boils down to is who gets my money when I'm gone."

"That will do for a start."

Lady Dinnister leaned forward slightly in her chair. The conversation seemed to be visibly aging her, and she made an obvious effort to order her thoughts and to speak clearly.

"I had only one child, Mr. Spence. A daughter, Vanessa. She died five years ago, which was a great blow to me. Vanessa, naturally, was my sole beneficiary, but when she died, I altered my will and divided most of what I shall leave between her two children, Elizabeth and Alec."

"Did you include your son-in-law?"

"No. He specifically asked to be left out."

"I don't believe I know his name."

"Edward. Edward Bannerman."

"Is he a man of some substance?"

"He has no private means, no. But he makes a fair living, and he has no great regard for money. He's an artist."

Spence's expression showed interest. "Ah yes, I thought the name rang a bell. I've seen some of his work."

"Don't misunderstand me, Mr. Spence. Edward lives pretty comfortably by most people's standards. He has a nice house, a couple of cars, I believe, and he travels quite a lot. But he has no yearning for conspicuous expenditure."

"Yes," said Spence. "I get the idea. So, to put it crudely, if inheriting wealth were a sufficient motive for murder, then your grandson and your granddaughter would be the chief suspects."

Lady Dinnister nodded. "That's about it, yes. Although I can't imagine that either of them would be capable of any such thing."

Spence made no comment. "Would you like to describe them to me?"

The old lady made another great effort of will. Laurel wondered how long his boss would go on pressing her.

"Well, I'll deal with Alec first. Alec is a very nice boy. I suppose all grandmothers say that, but it's true. He's twenty, he's taking a degree in engineering, and for the last few months he's been going about with my secretary, Susan Green."

"For the last few months, you say?"

"Yes."

"Are they engaged?"

"No, not yet."

"Will they be?"

"Possibly. But Alec still has another two years at university; he's on a four-year course."

"Would you object if they did become engaged?"

"No, not really. I think Alec could do rather better than settle for Susan, but that's for him to decide."

"Does Alec still live with his father?"

"Yes."

"I see. And what about Elizabeth?"

Lady Dinnister frowned and looked down. She paused before answering. "Well, I suppose if I am to be of any use to you, I must be frank."

"I think so."

"Well, if I say that Alec is a nice boy, then I suppose I must say that there is something not quite so attractive about Elizabeth. She is, of course, a perfectly normal and sensible person in many ways. But fundamentally, she is selfish. Spoilt, I suppose, in her childhood. She was very unhappy at boarding school too — I don't think she's ever quite got over it."

"Is she older or younger than Alec?"

"Older. She's twenty-six."

"Married?"

"Yes. She got married a couple of years ago to a man called Vernon Hassett."

"Any children?"

"No, and I don't think there will be. That's what I mean, you see. Selfish."

"What kind of a man is Vernon?"

Lady Dinnister almost smiled, but she was too deeply upset to smile properly. Her mouth moved slightly, temporarily relieving the sadness which marked her features. "Well, Vernon is quite an amusing man, in a totally unconscious way. He's young, perhaps a couple of years older than Elizabeth, but very pompous and not very bright."

"It sounds as if you don't like him much."

"Well, I try not to judge him too harshly. We've had words occasionally, but he's done me no great harm, and we all have our faults."

"What have you had words about?"

Lady Dinnister paused again, taking several deep breaths before she could speak in a firm voice.

"Mr. Spence, it's fortunate in a way that we have done business before. Because if I didn't know you and respect your professionalism, then I certainly wouldn't answer these questions."

"Believe me," said Spence, "it will save a great deal of time and trouble if you do. In a murder enquiry, nothing is sacred."

"Yes, well, I suppose you're right … What was it you asked me?"

"Your quarrel with Vernon Hassett," said Spence gently. "You were going to tell me what it was about."

"Oh yes. That … Well, it wasn't a quarrel, really — well, yes, I suppose it was … Anyway, what it boiled down to was this. Elizabeth and Vernon, they're a very extravagant couple, or so I believe. I doubt very much if they are living within their income. I said earlier that Edward wasn't interested in conspicuous expenditure, but his daughter and her husband certainly are. Cars, clothes, expensive holidays, you name it. There's no end to it, but that's the way they live, in a colour-supplement sort of world."

"And they've been after you for money?"

"Sort of. They've been trying to persuade me to sell Marlby Manor. To go and live somewhere smaller and cheaper."

"And pass the proceeds on now, rather than when you die?"

"Yes." Lady Dinnister looked up. "You seem almost psychic, Mr. Spence."

Spence smiled, "Not really. It's a fairly obvious line of thought. There would be tax advantages in it even if they weren't big spenders."

"Yes, well, no doubt you're right. Anyway, I've resisted the idea. For all sorts of reasons, logical and otherwise. I hate the thought of some Arab living in Marlby Manor, I really do. I've lived here all my married life, and I want to die here. But at the same time I realise that that is a selfish and subjective point of view. If I really want to do the best for my grandchildren — and I do — then I ought to do as they suggest, and sell up. So I feel selfish and guilty and unhappy."

"And that's what you fell out with Vernon about."

"Yes."

"Did all the family take his view?"

"Yes, they did, really. Edward and Alec and Elizabeth, they all seemed to agree. And I can see the strength of their argument. But I don't like it. I don't like it at all."

"What did Miss Fosdyke think you should do?"

"She told me I should stick to my guns. So I did."

Spence stood up and stretched his legs. He put his hands in his trouser pockets and walked about the room, his head lowered in thought. For a minute or two, he stared out of the window. Then he came back to his chair and sat down again.

Lady Dinnister seemed to have benefited from the break in the questioning; she looked very much more relaxed.

"Tell me about your staff," said Spence. "Is there anyone here who was with you at the time your silver was stolen ten years ago?"

Lady Dinnister thought back. "Well now, let me see. Only two, I think. Mr. McWinter, my head gardener, and Mrs. Jones, a part-time cleaner. That's all."

Spence nodded. "I see. So most of the present group of servants have joined you within the last ten years."

"Yes."

"How long has your secretary been working for you?"

"Oh, getting on for two years, I suppose."

"What does she do for you, apart from type letters? That can't take all day, surely."

"Well, no, it doesn't, but I do dictate a great deal at times — letters to old friends, you know. Anyway, apart from the typing, she also acts as a sort of administrative assistant. There's quite a lot to keep track of — insurances, maintenance work on the house, making my chequebook balance. All that sort of thing."

"She's a bit of a Girl Friday then?"

"Yes, you could say that."

"Is she efficient?"

"Oh yes, very."

"What's she like as a person?"

"Well, she's modest, unassuming, pleasant. She's a bit insecure, as you've no doubt noticed. And she's madly in love with my grandson, so that's making her a bit more sensitive than usual. All the pangs and heartaches of youth, you know."

"Yes," said Spence with a grin. "I remember. All right, let's leave her for the moment and go on to the butler, Mr. Tanner."

"Ah yes, dear old Tanner. Well, Tanner is a bit old and slow, like me. He'll soon be a pensioner, also like me. Miss Fosdyke used to say that he was lazy and that a younger man would do much more work for the same money. But it's not true that Tanner is lazy. He has more than a touch of arthritis, and that's no joke, I can assure you."

"So you're quite satisfied with his performance?"

"Oh yes. He's a good butler, and there aren't many of them left. They're a dying breed, you know."

"All right. What about Hazel?"

Lady Dinnister smiled. "I like Hazel. She's been a good friend to me in many ways, which is odd because we haven't much in common. She's loyal, hard-working, and an excellent cook."

"How do you mean, loyal?"

"Well, she doesn't gossip. There's no side to her. She doesn't say one thing to your face and another behind your back."

"She's a very attractive woman, despite her rather strange eyes. Is she spoken for?"

"Oh yes, very much so. She and my chauffeur share a flat over the garage at the rear of the house."

"In the old stables?"

"Yes."

"We saw your chauffeur polishing the car as we arrived this morning. What's his name?"

"Jones. Len Jones."

"Been here long?"

"Two years. He's a useful man. He likes to keep busy, and he does most of my painting and decorating. But he knows his limits; he won't touch electricity, for instance."

"Good references?"

"Yes, and he's lived up to them. Helpful, friendly, reliable. He and Hazel make a good pair, even if they haven't bothered to get married."

"But he's a good deal younger than her, isn't he?"

"Yes, about ten years, I should think. But that seems to be quite fashionable these days." Lady Dinnister's eyes twinkled with amusement. "I'm sure they'll stay together from now on."

"He looks as if he might have been a boxer."

"Possibly. You'll have to ask him. He's certainly done a bit of acting in his time."

"Amateur or professional?"

"Oh, bit parts in films, that sort of thing. Nothing very ambitious."

"Well now, are there any other staff?" asked Spence. "Or have we covered them all?"

"Well, there are two part-time cleaners, ladies from the village who come out and work under Hazel's direction. And then there's my gardener, Mr. McWinter, whom I've already mentioned, and a boy who works with him."

Spence nodded. "Do the gardeners report to you?"

"Not directly, no. I used to look after that sort of thing, but now I leave it all to Susan. She liaises with Mr. McWinter, and if there's any desperate decision to be made, I go down and take a look. Otherwise I let them get on with it. Mr. McWinter's judgement is usually a lot better than mine, anyway."

"Are there any antagonisms among your staff? Any rows, resentments, accusations?"

"Well, there are always occasional grumbles, but in the past few years we've had nothing to write home about." Lady Dinnister quoted from Stanley Holloway: "'No wrecks and nobody drownded. Fact nothing to laugh at at all.'"

Spence smiled; he was glad that Lady Dinnister had recovered her normal good spirits and that his questions were not proving too taxing.

"How many of your staff live in?" he asked.

"Three at the moment: Mr. Tanner, Hazel, and Len Jones. Miss Fosdyke was living in too, of course."

"Could I be very nosy and ask if you've left any money to them in your will?"

"I have, yes."

"Substantial sums?"

"Yes, I dare say you would think so. As I get older, I seem to need more help. I need good staff, so I offer them good wages, and by and large they stay. And if they stay, I feel it is only right to let them see a little light at the end of the tunnel."

"So they know they will receive some money when you die?"

"Yes. I think I've mentioned it to all of them at one time or another."

"Could I ask you how much you intend to leave them?"

"Yes, you may. And the answer is that my two longer-serving household staff will get about twenty-five thousand pounds each."

"That's Hazel and Mr. Tanner."

"Yes."

"And all the others proportionately less?"

"Yes. Depending on their length of service and, as I perceive it, their deserts."

"How did you determine that upper figure?"

"Well, it's the cost of a small house, more or less. In my lifetime, I can recall many an old retainer who became too elderly to go on working and had absolutely nowhere to go. It's all very well to say that they should think ahead and save up and so on, but with inflation being what it is, they'd never manage it. So it seems only right to help them out. And in case you're wondering, perhaps I ought to say that both my grandchildren will inherit many times that amount."

"Are there any other bequests, besides those to your servants and family?"

"Only to my doctor."

"Dr. Milton?"

"Yes. He's been very kind to me."

Spence rested his elbows on the arms of his chair and folded his hands in front of him. "I take it that you keep some sort of files on your household staff, with copies of their references, details of wages paid, and so forth?"

"Yes. Susan Green sees to all that."

"May I examine those files?"

"Yes, if you think it's important. Susan will show you where they are, and I'll make sure she knows you have my permission."

Spence nodded with satisfaction and stood up. "Good. Well, that's all for now, Lady Dinnister. I'm most grateful to you for talking to me at such length and for answering my questions so frankly."

Lady Dinnister sighed. "Well, I just hope it's been useful."

"I'd like to ask two further favours. First, I'd like to come back this afternoon and talk to your staff individually. And second, I'd like to send a team of forensic scientists along to go over Miss Fosdyke's room. I'll see that they don't make much disturbance, and after they've looked at the room, I shall want them to take everyone's fingerprints."

"My goodness," said Lady Dinnister. "Will they want my fingerprints, too?"

"Certainly."

"Oh, good." The lines on Lady Dinnister's face changed shape as she broke into an almost childishly gleeful smile. "I've never had my dabs taken before. I shall enjoy that."

*

Shortly afterwards Spence and Laurel left Marlby Manor and drove just over half a mile to the village of Marlby itself. Marlby was too small to be worthy of a police station, but there was a police house that had been built some fifteen years earlier to accommodate a constable for Marlby and the surrounding district. For the moment this house was unoccupied, so Spence had arranged for his detective sergeant, Percy Wilberforce, to set up an office for him in the front room. Sure enough, when Spence and Laurel arrived at the house, Wilberforce opened the door to greet them.

Percy Wilberforce was forty-two, a rather fierce-looking man with a short-back-and-sides haircut, a parting which looked as if it had been cut with a knife, and a small moustache. He habitually carried himself as if standing permanently to attention, largely because he was only just tall enough to meet the minimum requirement for the force. His military bearing was also reflected in the crisp crease in his trousers and the dazzling shine on his shoes. Despite the August sunshine, he was wearing a thick woollen sports jacket.

Wilberforce was normally based at the Police Headquarters Building in Wellbridge; his forte was administration, and he was in some respects the linchpin of the CID.

"Good afternoon," said Spence placidly. "All ready, are we?"

"Yes sir. This way, sir."

Wilberforce led the way into the front room of the house, where he had assembled chairs, tables, a telephone, files, pens, paper, and an electric kettle. For a moment Spence was tempted to ask where the kitchen sink was, but he didn't. It would have been unkind to tease a man for doing so precisely what he had been ordered to do.

"Good," said Spence, looking around. "Well, we seem to have all we need — let's get down to it."

The three men sat down, and while Laurel and Wilberforce began to prepare a few files for the statements which would shortly go in them, Spence made some phone calls.

First he arranged for the Southshire CID's Photographic and Fingerprint Department to call at Marlby Manor that afternoon. They would examine Miss Fosdyke's room thoroughly, photograph it, measure it, draw plans of it, and take note of any fingerprints, hairs, or fibres anywhere within it. After that they would take the fingerprints of all those who lived and worked in the manor and its grounds.

Next Spence telephoned the director of the local Home Office Regional Forensic Science Laboratory and arranged for Miss Fosdyke's bottle of sherry to be analysed. The typewritten compliments card was also to be studied and the typeface to be identified.

Finally Spence telephoned the chief constable to put him in the picture. He discovered that the chief constable was out — probably playing golf, Spence guessed — and left a message explaining what was going on.

Then, with the telephone calls out of the way, Spence began to write out some job cards.

The job-card system was by now well established in any murder investigation undertaken by the Southshire police. Spence, or the officer in charge, wrote out a job card for any item of work which needed to be done. The work was then allocated among the available men by Percy Wilberforce.

When the job was finished, the officer concerned wrote up a report. It was Wilberforce's duty to see that the reports were typed, read, and initialled by both Spence and Laurel. Once they had been read, the reports were indexed and filed.

The first job card that Spence wrote was for the firm of Williams and Williams to be asked if they actually had sent a complimentary bottle of sherry, which Spence thought extremely unlikely. However, a further check was to be made to see if any employees of Williams and Williams had had any connections with Lady Dinnister or Marlby Manor.

Finally Spence dictated an initial report on the case into his pocket-sized tape recorder and gave it to Wilberforce to be typed up. Copies would be sent to the chief constable and the county coroner.

After that Spence gathered the papers in front of him into a neat pile and looked up at Laurel.

"Hungry?" he asked.

"Yes, now you mention it."

"Good. Let's go and get some lunch."

Thirteen

Lunch was taken at the Fishmonger's Arms in Marlby and consisted mainly of bread and cheese, with draught Guinness for Spence and a lager for Laurel.

With lunch over, Spence rang his wife to tell her that he could not guarantee what time he would be home that night. After that he and Laurel drove back to Marlby Manor.

The afternoon heat was now quite intense, and they left their jackets and ties in the car.

The front door was opened to them by Mr. Tanner, who had certainly not shed *his* jacket and tie, and who raised a discreet eyebrow at their appearance as he admitted them.

"Good afternoon, gentlemen," said Tanner.

"Good afternoon," said Spence.

"A group of gentlemen from the CID arrived here a few minutes ago," Tanner continued.

"Yes. I saw their van outside."

"They're upstairs if you wish to see them."

"No, I don't think I will," said Spence, glancing up the stairs. "I think I'll leave them to it."

"Will you be wishing to see Lady Dinnister, sir?"

"No, not at the moment. We'll see Miss Green first."

The butler nodded. "Very well, sir. I'll show you her office."

Tanner moved off down a short corridor leading out of the hall. The two detectives followed him, and as he walked along behind the butler, Spence noticed that the man walked with a slight limp, favouring his right leg.

Tanner turned and indicated a door with the open palm of his hand. "Here you are, sir." And with that he seemed to melt tactfully and silently into the woodwork.

Spence knocked at the door. "Come in," said a voice, and he entered.

Susan Green turned from her seat at the typewriter, removing her reading glasses as she did so. "Oh," she said. "Superintendent Spence. It's you."

"Yes," said Spence.

Laurel closed the door behind him.

"Lady Dinnister said you would want to see me." Susan smiled nervously.

"Yes," said Spence again, in a tone which was neither friendly nor unfriendly; it was neutral, like his facial expression, allowing Miss Green to make of it what she would.

Spence and Laurel looked about, found two vacant chairs, and pulled them into a suitable position. They sat down.

"We shall be talking to all the staff at some time this afternoon," Spence continued.

"Yes, so I understand." Susan licked her lips. "Lady Dinnister" — Susan swallowed — "Lady Dinnister asked me to set aside a room for you to interview people in. So I have."

"That's very kind," said Spence, "but I don't suppose we shall use it. I prefer to see people in context, as it were. In your case, for instance, I shall talk to you in here, in your office."

Susan nodded. "Very well."

Spence studied the secretary thoughtfully before continuing. She was an attractive young woman — not beautiful, nor even pretty, because she lacked the radiant self-confidence needed for either attribute — but she had a good bone structure and a well-proportioned figure. She often seemed rather worried, and clearly felt self-conscious about her considerable height, but on those rare occasions when she smiled, her face lit up most pleasingly.

"It's quite a simple, straightforward procedure that we use," Spence told her. "My colleague and I will ask you some questions. When necessary, Mr. Laurel will take a few notes. Later on we shall get you to make a more formal statement, which will be written out and signed. For the record, you understand."

"Yes." The answer was accompanied by more nervous licking of the lips.

"Now then, first of all, I've been told that you keep files on all Lady Dinnister's employees. I'd like to see them, please."

"Yes, of course." Susan rose and crossed to a rather elderly green filing cabinet. She opened the top drawer and took out a number of manila folders.

"Thank you," said Spence as she passed the folders to him. "Have you included your own file?"

"Oh! No." Susan blushed and hurried back to the cabinet. "How silly of me." She extracted another folder and, by now thoroughly flustered, sat down with her knees pressed tightly together and her hands interlocked.

Spence let her wait for some time before beginning his questioning. He glanced idly through the pile of folders in his lap.

"How long have you been here?" he asked eventually.

"Um — nearly two years," said Susan.

"Do you enjoy it?"

"Oh yes. Very much."

"I find that a bit odd," said Spence. "I should have thought it was rather a dull job. Rather lonely. Not at all like a busy office in a city."

"Well," said Susan, "you're right about that. It's not a bit like a city job, that's true. But I tried that sort of thing once, and I didn't like it, so I was only too pleased to come here. And it's not a bit boring. On the contrary, it's very interesting because I'm given a lot to do, and a lot more interesting things than just typing letters."

"What sort of things?"

"Well, I tend to spend quite a lot of time on financial work. Lady Dinnister still makes all the decisions, of course, but I spend quite a lot of time talking to her lawyers and stockbrokers, things like that. And then I pay all the wages, look after the insurances, all that sort of thing."

"Yes, I see. What kind of typewriter have you got?"

Susan seemed temporarily thrown off balance by the sudden change of tack, which was exactly what Spence had intended; he never liked to let anyone get too comfortable. "What kind of typewriter?" Susan repeated.

"That's what I said."

"Oh. Well. It's an IBM. A golf-ball."

"What does that mean?"

"Well, it means that you can use different typefaces on it by changing the head. The heads looks just like golf balls. Here, I'll show you." Susan turned around to face her typewriter and lifted out the silver metal ball to show Spence.

Spence examined it. "Hmm. Useful," he said. "How many of these things have you got?"

"Two."

"Would you type 'the quick brown fox' with each of them, please?"

"Well, yes." Susan seemed puzzled but did as she was asked. "Here you are," she said when she had finished. She pulled the piece of paper out of the machine and passed it to Spence, who glanced at it briefly. He could see at once that the compliments slip from Williams and Williams had not been typed with either of these two typefaces.

"Twelve characters to the inch, I see," he said.

"Yes."

"Can the machine type at ten characters to the inch?"

"It can do, yes, but I haven't got the heads for that."

Spence nodded. "Who has access to this typewriter?"

"Well, anyone, I suppose. I mean I don't think anyone does use it except me, but they could if they wanted to."

"The door is always open?"

"Yes. I lock the filing cabinet, of course, but that's all."

"Who has keys to the cabinet?"

"Er, I have. And Lady Dinnister — she keeps one in her desk."

"How long have you had that ribbon in the typewriter?"

"Oh, about a week, I think."

"Take it out, please, and let Mr. Laurel have it."

"Oh. Yes, of course."

Susan turned around to the typewriter once again and then handed the extracted ribbon to Laurel, who popped it into the usual polyethylene bag.

"I gather Len Jones has done a bit of acting," said Spence, apparently referring to a file in his lap. "As a film extra."

"Um, yes, yes, I believe he has."

"Has he ever made a pass at you?"

Susan paused for a moment before replying. "Well, um, yes." She shifted her position uneasily. "As a matter of fact, he has."

"And what became of it?" Spence looked up into Susan's eyes, but she hastily glanced away.

"He's not my type, I'm afraid. Not my type at all."

Another pause. Then Spence changed his tack again. "I gather Hazel's a very good cook."

"Yes. Yes, she is."

"Is she friendly toward you?"

91

"Yes. Yes ... I like her."

"And what about Mr. Tanner?"

"Oh, we get on very well." Susan pushed her light brown hair back out of her eyes.

"But he's a rather elderly man, isn't he?"

"Yes. But I mean — what does that matter? He's perfectly friendly. We all get on well together."

"What kind of man is he?"

"Who — Mr. Tanner?"

"Of course."

"Well ... he keeps himself to himself. Does his work. Reads quite a lot, I believe. He's a good employee."

"Was Miss Fosdyke a good employee?"

"Oh, she wasn't an employee."

"Wasn't she? Didn't she get paid?"

"Oh yes, yes, of course. That's not what I meant."

"You mean she was treated slightly differently from the others."

"Yes. Yes. She was a companion. A sort of friend, really."

"But more of an equal to Lady Dinnister than an employee?"

"Yes. Precisely."

"How did you get on with her?"

"Well, if you must know, I didn't really like her all that much."

"Why not?"

"Well, she was a bit bossy. A bit fierce. Rather inclined to think she knew best about everything."

"How did she feel about you and Alec Bannerman?"

Susan's cheeks coloured, but not too intensely; she was beginning to get used to Spence and his questions.

"Um, well — she didn't seem to approve."

"And did she say so?"

"Yes. Quite nicely, but she did say that Alec was too young to be getting serious about anyone."

"Why would anyone want to kill Lady Dinnister?"

"Lady Dinnister?"

"Yes."

Susan paused again. She had a habit, Spence noticed, of repeating his question whenever she needed time to think.

92

"I really can't imagine."

"Don't lie to me," said Spence amicably. "You've been very honest up to now — transparently honest, one might say. So don't change your habits now."

"I — I can't think what you mean," stammered Susan. Her eyes looked hurt and frightened by Spence's change of manner.

"What I mean," said Spence, "is that any normal person could think of several reasons why people should want to kill Lady Dinnister. So you *can* imagine; you can imagine very easily. And I want you to start. Now."

Susan twisted her hands together anxiously. There was a long, desperate silence.

"Well," she said at last, "I suppose someone might want to kill her for revenge. Or money … Or because they were mad."

"Good," said Spence. "That's better. Let's take revenge as a motive. What has Lady Dinnister done that would cause anyone to seek revenge?"

"I don't know," said Susan, her voice cracking slightly with strain. "I really don't."

"Think," Spence instructed her. "Lady Dinnister has had a long and active life. She's bound to have offended and hurt some people. Who? In what way?"

Susan's eyes began to fill with tears.

"What is Lady Dinnister capable of?" Spence persisted. "What dreadful secrets could she have?"

"I don't know," Susan whispered. "I really don't know."

Silence descended once more, and Spence sat and waited. He knew that he could endure silence far more readily than those whom he questioned, but he had to wait a long time before Susan Green looked up. When she did so, it was obvious that tears from both eyes had overflowed and run down her cheeks.

"Well?" said Spence.

"Perhaps … perhaps Lady Dinnister might have stolen someone's sweetheart."

"Stolen someone's sweetheart," Spence repeated sonorously, as if trying it out for sound. "Yes, that is entirely possible. In her younger days, she might have seduced someone's husband, and that person might have hated her for it. You think that's likely, do you?"

"No, no, not at all!" Susan was deeply shocked. "But you asked me to think of possibilities."

"Indeed I did. Have you heard any rumours of that sort?"

"Absolutely not."

"But Lady Dinnister is, or was, capable of that sort of thing?"

"Well … I don't think she would ever have done anything wicked or unkind. But she is a very strong and determined lady."

"Is she strong and determined enough to be leaving you anything in her will?"

Despite her tears and fluster, Susan looked up at Spence sharply. "No, not as far as I know."

"What about the other household staff — is she leaving them anything?"

"Well, yes, I believe she is. Hazel, and Mr. Tanner. Lady Dinnister is a very generous person."

"Which of the other household staff are capable of murder?"

Susan's face twisted in revulsion. "That's an absolutely horrible question."

"Nevertheless, I want an answer."

"None of them. None of them is capable of murder."

"That's not true," said Spence. "Almost all of us are capable of murder if pressed hard enough, as you would agree if you thought about it properly. Now, which of the household staff would need the least pressing? And think before you answer."

Susan fidgeted and squirmed on her chair until perhaps half a minute had elapsed. "Well, if you must have an answer, I suppose Len Jones."

"Why him?"

"Because he's less civilised than all the rest. More of a caveman. I believe he used to do some boxing, and boxers are supposed to have a killer instinct, aren't they? But, in any case, none of us *needs* to kill Lady Dinnister."

"Why not?"

"Because she's old, and she'll die soon anyway." Susan glanced at Spence and saw that he had raised an eyebrow in doubt, so she went on to justify her statement. "Oh, I know she looks pretty fit to you. She always perks up a lot when there's company about — particularly men. But the fact is that she's ill more often than not. She's old and tired, and visibly fading. The doctor comes quite frequently."

"Ah yes," said Spence thoughtfully. "The worthy Dr. Milton ... Are you going to see Alec this evening?"

"Alec?"

"Your lover," said Spence bluntly. He was by now very tired of Susan Green's evasiveness. "Are you going to see him tonight?"

"Oh. Yes. Yes, I expect I am."

Spence nodded. "That's all, Miss Green. You may go now."

As if hardly able to believe her ears, Susan Green stood up, hesitated for a moment, and then left the room, closing the door after her.

Spence sat and stared at the files in his lap for a moment or two. Laurel added a line to his notes before speaking. "Well," he said as he closed his notebook for the time being, "you were a bit hard on her, weren't you?"

"What?" said Spence. "That poor young slip of a girl who's only five-foot-nine and twenty-four years old? Hard on her, you mean?"

"Yes. A bit."

"Well," said Spence, "perhaps I was. But murder is a serious business, and it was her misfortune to be seen first. Whoever was seen first in this household was going to get a rough ride because I want the word to go round that we mean business."

"It will do that all right," said Laurel.

"In any case, she struck me as being a rather oversensitive young woman. Almost suspiciously so."

"Do you think she has a motive?"

"What for?"

"Trying to kill Lady Dinnister."

"Yes. She certainly does. By all accounts she's madly in love with Alec Bannerman, and with his grandmother dead he'd be a very rich man."

"But she says that the old lady is due to depart fairly soon without any help."

"Which may or may not be true. I always remember the case of a district nurse in Wellbridge who was retired due to ill health at the age of fifty-six, and lived to be a hundred and two."

Laurel grinned. "Yes, I remember reading about her, too."

Spence glanced at his watch. "Well, I think we'll just read through these folders until Miss Green has had time to spread the word about what a dreadful fellow I am, and then we'll go and see someone else."

Fourteen

The two detectives wandered through the ground-floor corridors of the manor for some time until eventually they found themselves in the kitchen.

The kitchen was large, with a very old table in the centre; the top of the table had turned white and was ridged from frequent scrubbing. Around the perimeter of the room were large areas of waist-high formica working surfaces, with spacious cupboards below. There were further cupboards fixed higher up the walls on two sides of the room.

There was no one to be found in the kitchen, but through an open window Spence could just see the back of hazel's head as she sat outside in the sunshine. He went out through the back door and found her sunning herself in a white metal chair on a small verandah. She was sitting with the back of her head resting on the top of the chair, soaking up the sunshine. A cup of tea was on the metal table in front of her. She looked extremely relaxed.

"Do you mind if we join you?" Spence asked as he approached.

Hazel opened her eyes and brought her chin down to look at him directly. "If you must," she said.

"What about a cup of tea for two hard-working detectives?"

"What about it?"

"We'd like one," said Spence. He sat down on one of the three vacant chairs around the table, and Laurel occupied another one.

"Hmm!" said Hazel in an unfriendly tone, and she sighed heavily at what she clearly considered to be yet another example of typical male selfishness. But after a moment she got up, disappeared into the kitchen, and emerged shortly with two cups of tea and a sugar bowl. Spence and Laurel thanked her warmly and then sat and sipped their tea gratefully while Hazel resumed her seat.

"Very nice," said Spence in due course. "Very nice indeed."

"You could do a lot worse,'* said Hazel. "A lot worse." Though whether she was talking about the tea, the weather, or something else was not clear.

"What did you think of Miss Fosdyke?" Spence asked her.

Hazel did not seem at all disturbed by his sudden question. "She was all right," she said simply.

"Just that?"

"Yes."

"What did the other household staff think of her?"

"Why don't you ask them?"

"Oh, I will," said Spence earnestly. "I will ... Did Miss Fosdyke strike you as the suicidal type?"

Hazel snorted. "You must be joking."

"You mean no, do you?"

"Of course I mean no," said Hazel sharply. "She was as strong as a bloody horse."

"Physically or mentally?"

"Both. She would have lived to be ninety if someone hadn't poisoned her."

"Ah yes. And speaking of poison, what did Miss Fosdyke have to eat on Monday?"

Hazel gave him a look that would have made most men take three steps backwards. "Now look here, you," she said cuttingly, demonstrating that she was not one to be intimidated by any mere Detective Chief Superintendent. "I don't know who you bloody think you are, but if you think you can go around suggesting that Miss Fosdyke died because of something I cooked for her, then all I can suggest is that you go away and come back later when I've got my lawyer present."

Spence held up his hand with his palm facing towards her. "Hazel, Hazel, my dear girl," he murmured soothingly, "nothing could be further from my thoughts, I assure you." He put down his cup for the moment so that he could concentrate on easing the deep furrows from Hazel's brow. "I am not suggesting for one instant that Miss Fosdyke died of food poisoning. On the contrary, I am quite certain that she didn't — at least, not in the accepted sense of the term. I know very well that Miss Fosdyke died because someone deliberately poisoned her. But the question is bound to be asked, and I ask it now — what did Miss Fosdyke have to eat on the day before she died?"

Hazel seemed mollified. "Hmm, well. If you put it like that ... "

Spence inclined his head to indicate that he did indeed put it like that. He resumed drinking his tea.

Hazel pondered. "Well, let me see. Breakfast was cornflakes and kippers. Coffee. More coffee mid-morning. Lunch was cold beef and salad, followed by cheese and biscuits. No wine, but a cup of tea afterwards, I seem to remember. In the evening we had something a bit more elaborate. They had tomato juice to start with, and then I did trout with almonds."

"What sort of vegetables?"

"Nothing very exotic. Peas and potatoes."

"And for dessert?"

"I made a fruit salad. Fresh fruit with cream."

"Coffee?"

"Yes. They both had coffee."

"'Both' being Miss Fosdyke and Lady Dinnister."

"Yes."

"Anything to drink with the dinner?"

"Well, if I remember rightly, they shared the remnants of a bottle of white wine. Not much; about a glass each. Chablis, I think it was, but not a very good one."

"What about nightcaps later on?"

"I wouldn't know, I'm afraid. I didn't make them anything, I can tell you that."

"Miss Fosdyke didn't eat any shellfish that day?"

"No."

"You're sure?"

"Well, as sure as I can reasonably be. I didn't serve her any, put it like that."

Spence sat back in his chair; the sun was almost uncomfortably hot. "It sounds to me as if Lady Dinnister likes good cooking."

"She likes life," said Hazel. "It's as simple as that. Oh, I know she's not so mobile now — not so good on her feet as she was. But she used to be a very strong, active woman, with a good, healthy appetite. And she still has a tremendous range of interests; she's involved with a list of charities as long as your arm, and streams of people come to see her."

Spence was silent for a moment, thinking. "Do you do all the cooking?" he asked.

"Yes. Well, all except a few sauces. Mr. Tanner does those."

"Why?"

"Well, it's a sort of tradition, isn't it? Butlers always do sauces, or always used to, at any rate. They're very secretive about it, never let you see what they put in them. The recipes are passed on from father to son in some cases."

"I see." Spence was intrigued. "Did Mr. Tanner do a sauce for the trout?"

"No. I did. I could do them all, of course. In fact, I could do them a darn sight better than Tanner, but it keeps him happy and makes him think he's useful. That's what you have to do with men, you know — keep them happy."

Spence smiled. "Yes," he said, "I'm sure you're right there ... Now then, think about this one. Who do you know who hates Lady Dinnister badly enough to want to murder her?"

Hazel looked at him in surprise. "Are you sure you mean Lady Dinnister?"

"Yes."

"Oh," said Hazel. Then she sighed heavily.

"Why do you sigh?"

"Because it's a bloody stupid question, if you want my opinion."

"Is it?"

"Of course it is. No one hates her enough to do that."

"But it rather looks as though someone did."

"I doubt it."

"She's lived a long time," Spence persisted. "She's seventy-two. She must have trodden on a few toes somewhere along the line."

"I expect she has. We all have. But not enough for anyone to want to murder her. Surely not."

"What about her grandchildren?"

"Well, they certainly wouldn't do it — neither of them."

"But they stand to gain a small fortune when she dies — in fact, a large fortune, from what I hear."

Hazel was growing irritated. "Yes, but they would never, never try to kill her. I keep telling you."

"But this girl Elizabeth is supposed to be a nasty piece of work."

"Well, you could say that. And if you did, I wouldn't argue very hard with you. But she hasn't got it in her to kill anyone. That's a different league altogether."

"What about her husband?"

Hazel put back her head and roared with laughter. "Him? Vernon? He couldn't say boo to a goose. He hasn't got the nerve."

"And the grandson, Alec Bannerman?"

Hazel shook her head. "No, no, no. He's a quiet lad. A nice boy. He goes to university."

It was Spence's turn to sigh. "Maybe so," he said. "But unfortunately, our prisons are full of people who went to university. They're just as criminal as the rest of us — only a bit more subtle about it."

"You're wrong, you know," Hazel continued. "Wrong about the whole thing. Nobody would try to kill Lady Dinnister, not for money or for anything else. She's not nasty enough to deserve it. And, in any case, it wasn't Lady Dinnister who got poisoned; it was Miss Fosdyke."

"Ah, yes," said Spence, "but the awkward fact of the matter is that someone put poison into a bottle of sherry that was intended as a gift for Lady Dinnister."

Hazel looked at him shrewdly. "Are you sure about that?"

"I'm quite sure that Miss Fosdyke was poisoned, yes. And I'm fairly sure that the poison was in a bottle of sherry and that the sherry was intended for Lady Dinnister. It had a compliments slip with it, addressed to Lady Dinnister, from Williams and Williams, wine merchants."

Hazel snorted derisively. "I don't believe it."

"What don't you believe?"

"That Williams and Williams would send us a free bottle of sherry. Wine merchants just don't do that sort of thing. Not anymore."

"But that's precisely my point," said Spence. "Someone bought a bottle of sherry, doctored it, and sent it round with a note saying it was for Lady Dinnister."

Hazel digested that information at length. "And you mean Fosdyke drank it by mistake?" she asked slowly. Spence nodded.

Hazel shook her head. "Well, I never saw it," she said thoughtfully, staring down at the ground as she searched her memory. "I see most of the stuff that comes in here, certainly anything like that. But I never saw that bottle of sherry."

"So you don't know how that particular bottle came to be in Miss Fosdyke's room?"

"No. No idea."

"Where do you buy your sherry, normally?"

"At the supermarket. Cheapest place, naturally. I can spend what I like on food, within reason, but we don't throw money about for the sake of it. No one does these days."

Spence shifted position in his chair. He was anxious to move on and talk to someone else, but there was one other point he wanted to clear up. "Tell me about this hair-dryer business."

Hazel laughed shortly. "Oh — that."

"What happened?"

"Well, it gave me an electric shock, didn't it?"

"Had you used it before?"

"Oh yes. Loads of times."

"And you'd had no problems?"

"No, none at all."

"Why do you think it gave you a shock last Friday?"

"Well, I think it just got a bit too old, that's all. We should have known, really; it was a very old-fashioned model."

"Lady Dinnister says she took it to pieces, and it seemed to her that someone had deliberately scraped the cover off a live wire."

"Yes, I've heard her say that myself, but I think she's wrong. It just wore out, that's all."

"Where is the hair-dryer now?"

"It's in the kitchen, as a matter of fact. I was thinking of throwing it out."

"Good job you haven't," said Spence. "I'll take it from you in a minute." He rose to his feet. "Tell me, have you seen the men checking out Miss Fosdyke's room?"

"Yes, of course I've seen them. They're all over the bloody place, aren't they?"

"Make them a cup of tea a bit later on, Hazel, there's a good girl."

"Hmm!" said Hazel with a sniff. "I'll think about it."

Fifteen

According to Hazel, Mr. Tanner was probably to be found in his room at the far end of the east wing, on the first floor, so after collecting the hair-dryer, Spence and Laurel next made their way upstairs.

As they passed Miss Fosdyke's bedroom, they paused to see how the photographic and fingerprint work was progressing; all seemed to be proceeding normally, so they moved on to interview Mr. Tanner.

"Come in," called Tanner at Spence's second knock on the door. The first knock had been drowned by the sound from the television set that could be heard from inside the room.

As he entered, Spence could see that the twenty-one-inch colour television was showing horse racing. Tanner looked back over his shoulder from his chair, and as soon as he realised who was visiting him, he immediately turned down the volume of the race commentary with his remote-control switch and rose awkwardly to his feet.

"Oh, it's you, sir. Please come in."

Tanner had been sitting in his shirtsleeves, but he now pulled his jacket on, as if he felt it was important to look smart when being interviewed by the police.

Spence and Laurel entered the room, closing the door behind them, and Tanner crossed to the television set to turn it off completely. He took his time over this manoeuvre since he was clearly interested in seeing the result of the race in progress, but as the horses passed the post and began to slow down to a canter, he flicked off the set without comment.

"On a winner there, were you?" asked Spence.

The butler grinned ruefully. "No, but Lady Dinnister was."

"Oh, she has a bet, does she?"

"Now and then. yes. Mostly when she's bored or upset. Takes her mind off things, you know."

"Yes. And you follow the form too, do you?"

"Oh yes." Tanner jangled some coins in his trouser pocket, looking a bit defensive. "I have a bet most days. Adds a little spice to life."

"Yes indeed," said Spence, looking around the room. "Yes indeed ... Well, sit down, Mr. Tanner, sit down. We'd just like to ask you a few questions."

"Yes, yes, of course." The butler hitched up his trousers and lowered his bulky frame back into the easy chair. "And the same to you, gentlemen — please make yourselves comfortable." With his hand he indicated two other chairs in the room.

"Thanks," said Spence. "I will in a minute."

Laurel sat down and began to jot down the time and circumstances in his notebook. Spence crossed to the windows and looked out to the east. Some yards away he could see a high wall, and beyond it an extensive kitchen garden; it was not one of the more attractive views from the manor, which was presumably why the room had been allocated to a member of staff.

The room itself, however, was large and elegantly furnished, mostly with art nouveau furniture that had seen better days. On the far side, away from the window, was a bed. There was also a large wardrobe, a table, and half a dozen chairs of varying shapes and sizes. But apart from a newspaper open at the racing page and a small selection of books on a shelf, there was scarcely a sign that the room was occupied at all; there were no mementoes, no framed photographs — not even a hairbrush on top of the chest of drawers. Mr. Tanner appeared to be a man of both few possessions and exceptionally tidy habits.

"Have you lived in this room long?" asked Spence.

"Oh, four or five years."

"And how do you like this style of furniture?" said Spence, examining a chair which might have been designed by Charles Rennie Mackintosh himself.

"Oh, I don't notice it really." The butler shrugged. "You can get used to anything after a bit."

"Yes," said Spence thoughtfully. "I suppose you can." He returned the chair to its former position and sat down on it. "I see you're a bit of a reader, Mr. Tanner."

"What, the books, you mean?"

"Yes."

"Well, I go to the library most weeks. Read anything, really."

"Particularly cookery."

"Well, yes. I mean, that's my job really, isn't it? Knowing a bit about people's stomachs. How to keep them happy. Sauces really, that's what I'm most interested in. And sport. I read quite a lot about sport, and watch it on the box."

The butler's left hand moved nervously up and down the side of his face as he looked at Spence. Like many people who are not used to contact with the police, he seemed decidedly ill at ease.

"Well, now," said Spence, who seemed very comfortable himself, "what we've come to see you about, of course, is the death of Miss Fosdyke."

"Ah yes, yes," said Tanner, lowering his hands to his lap and glancing quickly from Spence to Laurel and back again. "Terrible business, that. Terrible. Terrible."

"How did you get on with Miss Fosdyke personally?"

"Who, me?"

"Yes."

"Oh, very well. Very well indeed. A very nice lady. Miss Fosdyke was. One of the old school. I feel very cut up about this whole business. Really upset me, it has. The only good thing you can say about it is that it wasn't Lady Dinnister."

"How do you mean?"

"Well, it was meant for her, wasn't it? This poison?" Tanner glanced anxiously from face to face again.

"Ah yes, I see what you mean."

"In the sherry, I understand," Tanner continued. "That's wicked, that is. Really wicked. And she likes a drop of sherry too, does Lady Dinnister. In fact, she's a good judge of wine all around — remarkably good, for a woman." He paused, his fingers tapping together in the air in front of him.

"The sherry seems to have come from Williams and Williams," said Spence. "A complimentary bottle. Do you remember it being delivered?"

"Williams and Williams?" said Tanner. "No, I can't say I do. Don't think we've ever ordered anything from them. And certainly not a complimentary bottle. I'd remember that all right — like snow in July."

"Who do you know who hates Lady Dinnister?" asked Spence quietly.

The butler looked shocked. "Oh, well, no one hates her. Not Lady Dinnister. That's a bit too strong."

"Is it?" said Spence. "Do you mean to tell me that Lady Dinnister has gone all the way through a long and active life without offending someone somewhere?"

"Oh, well, I suppose there have been words exchanged now and then."

"Strong words?"

"Well, yes."

"For instance?"

"Well — off the top of my head — there was a row with Miss Goldman up at the golf club. Can't remember what it was about now. Something about a free lunch for those helping out at a tournament, something like that. Oh, we all have rows now and then, don't we? But we don't go around killing each other and hating each other afterwards."

"Well, unfortunately, some of us do," said Spence mildly. "Is Lady Dinnister ever sharp with the staff?"

"Oh, now and then, yes. But you've got to be, haven't you, in her position? Got to maintain some discipline, some standards. Otherwise people get slack."

"Was she ever short-tempered with Miss Fosdyke?"

"Oh, they got on each other's nerves from time to time. But they'd be bound to, wouldn't they? Two women spending the whole day together. But it never meant very much. And Lady Dinnister has a lot of pain, you know. Well, you wouldn't know, not knowing her very well. But you can always tell when she's in pain because she lashes out with her tongue. And then you have to persuade her to have some of her pills, as tactfully as possible, and after that she's her normal self again. Pain makes villains of us all, you know."

"Have you got any brothers or sisters, Mr. Tanner?"

The butler seemed totally thrown by the unexpectedness of the question. He could see no logical connection between that and what had gone before, and he looked almost desperately toward Laurel for guidance. But Laurel kept his eyes on his notebook, so there was nothing for it but to answer the question as put.

"Um, no," he said. "No brothers and sisters. No close family at all, as a matter of fact."

"And you've been in service all your life?"

"Yes. Well, more or less. Apart from the war, you know."

"What did you do in the war?"

"Well, I was in the army, like everyone else. Came out a sergeant."

"See any action?"

"Oh yes, lots. Too much, really. Dunkirk, D-Day — you name it, I was there."

"So, apart from that, you've never done anything else other than be a butler?"

"Oh yes. There are always odd periods between jobs, you know."

"Such as?"

"Well, I ran a shop for a couple of years. Village post office. Didn't like the life, though."

"Why not?"

"Well, you work terribly long hours, and you're at everyone's beck and call the whole time."

"Sounds a bit like being a butler to me," said Spence with a grin.

"No, it's not. Believe me, sir, it's quite different."

"What about marriage?"

"Oh, well, I was married once. Divorced, I'm afraid." The butler grinned nervously.

"Have you ever worked on a farm?"

"No. No, I can't say I have."

"What about Lady Dinnister's chauffeur, Mr. Jones — has he ever worked on a farm?"

The butler glanced at Laurel again; here was yet another of those funny questions, he seemed to be saying. How on earth am I supposed to know that? This time Laurel met his gaze with a perfectly blank expression.

The butler returned his attention to Spence. "I wouldn't know," he said helplessly. "I'm afraid you'll have to ask Len. I have a game of snooker with him, now and then, of an evening, but I don't know nothing about his background."

But then inspiration dawned. "I tell you what, though," Tanner continued, ever the helpful butler. "I can tell you who has worked on a farm this summer. Young Alec, Mr. Bannerman's boy."

"Lady Dinnister's grandson?"

"Yes, him. He's as brown as a berry. He's a student, of course, up at university, but he's been working on a farm in his vacation."

"Thank you," said Spence. "That's very useful to know. And what do you plan to do when you retire, Mr. Tanner?"

"Oh, I'm not going to retire," said the butler cheerfully, all smiles now. "Good heavens, no."

"But you're of an age to retire soon," said Spence gently. "Nearly sixty-five, aren't you?"

"Oh well, yes, but you're as young as you feel — that's what I always say. And I feel pretty good."

"What about your leg, Mr. Tanner? I notice you limp a bit. Is that an old war wound?"

"Well, no, it isn't really. It's a touch of arthritis, as a matter of fact. But it's not too bad in the summer, and the doctor tells me that if it gets really bad, they can always give me a new hip, so I'm not too worried about that." He beamed and rubbed the arms of his chair.

"So with a bit of luck, Mr. Tanner, you'll stay here for as long as Lady Dinnister needs a butler?"

"Yes. Yes, I suppose you could say that. You never know what's going to happen, of course, but I'm very happy here."

"And where would you go when the time does come to leave?"

"Well, I don't know. Get a little cottage somewhere, I suppose."

"You haven't bought anywhere yet, then?"

"No, no, but I've had my eye on one or two places."

Spence rose to his feet and stretched himself. He wandered over to the windows and stood leaning out, his hands resting on the windowsill.

"That's a very large kitchen garden out there," he said. "And the grounds are bigger still." He turned to face into the room again. "I should think weeds must be a bit of a problem, wouldn't you, Mr. Tanner?"

The butler floundered and said nothing. He looked as if his dearest wish was that this detective would stop asking him questions that he didn't quite understand.

Sixteen

A few minutes later Spence and Laurel left Mr. Tanner to get on with watching the races. They themselves went downstairs in search of Len Jones.

They found him up a ladder at the side of the house, painting a window frame. As they paused at the bottom of his ladder, Jones looked down at them, gathered that they wanted a word, and came down to greet them, paint pot in hand.

"You timed that well," Jones told them cheerfully. "I'd just finished." He carefully wiped his brush on the side of the tin of paint and laid it on some newspaper. "You're police, aren't you?" he enquired, looking up at them and squinting into the sun.

Spence nodded.

"Thought you'd be round to see me before long. Shan't be a minute."

Spence and Laurel stepped to one side while Jones methodically tidied up. He put the lid on the tin of paint, washed his brush with white spirit and water, and finally wiped his hands clean on a piece of rag.

"Right," he said when he was ready. "Let's go inside, shall we?"

Jones led the way across the yard at the back of Marlby Manor and entered what had once been the stable block. He went up a narrow flight of stairs and ushered the two detectives into what was evidently the living room of a spacious, well-furnished flat.

"Take a seat, gentlemen," said Jones. "I'll just get out of these overalls."

He disappeared and emerged perhaps two minutes later, wearing a casual sports shirt, jeans, and a pair of old felt slippers.

"There," he said, sitting down opposite Spence. "That's better. Now — what can I do for you?"

Spence looked around him. "Nice place you've got here."

"Yes, very nice. Very nice indeed."

"How long have you been working at the manor?"

"Oh, a couple of years. Two years in September."

"And how long has Hazel lived here with you?"

Jones took the question in his stride. "A year. Just over. She moved across from the main house last July."

Spence nodded. "Is this furniture yours?"

"Some of it. Some of it's Hazel's. I used to have a flat in Streatham, but I gave it up after a bit and had my stuff sent down here. Most of it, anyway. Some of it's in store."

"And where did Hazel's furniture come from?"

"Oh, most of it she got when she was married, I think. She had a pub once, she and her husband, but he drank away most of the profits, I gather, so she divorced him."

"Do you drink, Mr. Jones?"

"Now and again. All things in moderation, that's what I say." He smiled cheerfully.

Spence crossed his legs. "Tell me about yourself, Mr. Jones."

"What, background and that?"

"Yes."

"All right. Well, age twenty-nine, born South London, lived there most of my life. Left school at sixteen, had lots of odd jobs, didn't like any of 'em much until I got into chauffeuring."

"What about sport?"

"Oh, well, I've done most things. Football, cricket, boxing, wrestling. Even been a male model. I'm still on the books of an agency."

"Were you ever a professional boxer?"

"Yes — for seven fights."

"Why didn't you go on with it?"

"Well, I didn't have the class for it, did I? Same with football and wrestling. Never quite good enough to get to the top, you see. And you have to have a bit of class, otherwise you're just somebody's punching bag. And that's not good for your 'ealth." He grinned uninhibitedly. "And anyway, my jaw sticks out too far for a boxer." He roared with laughter, apparently quite unconcerned by the presence of the law.

Spence smiled back. "What's your ambition now, Mr. Jones?"

"Well, we'd like to have a place of our own, Hazel and me. We're saving hard."

"What kind of a place?"

"Well, a restaurant perhaps, or a small hotel."

"Not a pub?"

"No, not really. I suppose we could get one easy enough, but it doesn't appeal. No, we'd like something with a bit more class, a restaurant or a boardinghouse, as I say. I'm not the brightest bloke in the world, I know that. But thicker blokes than me have done all right in business. And Hazel's a dab hand with the food."

"Yes," said Spence. "I'm sure you're right."

"Plough back the profits at first," said Jones. "That's the secret. Too many people flash the money around, you know, that's where they go wrong."

"You said a minute ago that you've done a bit of modelling. What about part-time acting?"

"Oh yes, I've been an extra many a time, for films and TV and whatnot."

"Done much recently?"

"No, not while I've been down here. It's not convenient, really. Lady Dinnister needs me as a driver most days. But sometimes, when she's away on holiday, or not feeling too well, now and again it works out."

"How do you get on with Lady Dinnister?"

"Very well, thanks. No trouble at all."

"How did you get on with Miss Fosdyke?"

"Oh so-so. We didn't have much in common, really."

"This seems to me," said Spence, "to be a rather small, enclosed sort of household. Rather isolated. Surely you must get on each other's nerves, don't you?"

"Oh, there've been one or two rows, yes. Hazel and one of the cleaners had a fight, I remember. The cleaner left in the end. And I didn't get on well with one of the gardeners. He left in the end, too!" Jones roared with laughter once again. "Since then it's all been quite peaceful."

"Tell me about the wheel coming off Lady Dinnister's car."

Jones looked disconcerted for the first time and tugged at his ear. "Oh, that, yes. Well, that was very embarrassing. Very embarrassing indeed."

"In what way?"

"Well, I'm supposed to take care of her, aren't I? Keep the old lady away from traffic accidents and that. And actually, the wheel didn't come right off, you know, it just came loose."

"Why was that?"

"Well, it's my belief that when the car was in for a service, the garage just didn't tighten it up properly."

"Did you go back and complain?"

"You bet your life I did. I made a bloody great fuss about it. And the bloke swore blind that everything had been double-checked when the car left him."

"Did you believe him?"

"No." Jones grinned.

"Could the wheel have been loosened on purpose, do you think?"

"No." Jones was scornful. "Who would have done that?"

"I don't know," said Spence. "But somebody poisoned Miss Fosdyke."

Jones rubbed his enormous jaw reflectively. "Oh yes," he grunted. "I see what you mean."

After a few more minutes talking to Len Jones, Spence headed toward the kitchen garden, which he had seen from the window of the butler's room.

"I want to have a look at the gardener's shed," he told Laurel.

"Do you want me to check up on this garage business?" asked Laurel as they walked along a gravel path.

"Yes, you'd better. Get someone to press them really hard. Did they really double-check the wheels on that Rolls, or were they just plain sloppy? And also that bouquet with the barbed wire on it. Get that checked out too — was it carelessness, or could it conceivably have been deliberate?"

"Seems a very odd way to try to kill someone if it was deliberate."

"Well, you never know," said Spence. "Stranger things have happened at sea. And I suppose an old lady could die of blood poisoning or lockjaw or something without attracting much attention. Oh — and make sure that Hazel has handed over that hair dryer to Forensic."

They arrived at the gardener's shed, a large wooden structure forming an island in a sea of vegetables. The door was open, and the two detectives went inside.

The interior was burning hot, the result of several hours of unbroken August sunshine. Spence blinked as his eyes got used to the reduced light level.

"I suppose we're looking for weedkiller, are we?" asked Laurel.

"That's right."

For a minute or two, Spence and Laurel poked around among the bags of fertiliser, sacks of grass seed, and tins of creosote. The shed seemed to be a dumping ground for several generations of gardening produce and equipment. Before long, however, a shadow fell across the door.

"Can I help you, gentlemen?" asked a strong Scots voice in an aggressive tone, which suggested that help was the very last thing the speaker had in mind.

"What you really mean," said Spence, looking up, "is what the hell are we doing here?"

"Aye, if you insist."

Spence took out his warrant card and held it up. "Detective Chief Superintendent Spence and Detective Inspector Laurel. We're here to make enquiries into the death of Miss Emily Fosdyke."

"Oh. Are you now? Well, I suppose that's different."

"I hope so," said Spence. "You're Mr. McWinter, I suppose?"

"Aye, that's right."

McWinter was about sixty, Spence judged, a bearded man with fierce dark eyes and no doubt a hot temper to match. He wore a pair of very elderly corduroy trousers tied up with string, a faded striped shirt with the sleeves rolled up, a neckerchief to mop up the sweat around his neck, and a broad-brimmed hat. He was not a heavily built man by any means, but his brown arms were thick and strong.

"I'd like you to tell me what kind of weedkiller you use, Mr. McWinter."

"Why do you want to know that?"

"None of your business," said Spence amicably. "Just answer the question."

Mr. McWinter stayed put in the doorway for a moment, giving Spence a strange look, but then he came forward and advanced on one of the shelves.

"Well, we use all kinds. Are you looking for anything in particular?"

"Sodium arsenite," said Spence.

"Arsenic, is it?" McWinter paused. "There's much more deadly stuff than that around now, you know."

"Never mind. That's what I want to see."

With a shrug, McWinter lifted down an old paint tin, about twelve inches in diameter and six inches tall. He pried off the lid with a piece of wood.

"There y'are."

Spence looked inside. The tin was about two-thirds full of white powder. "You buy it wholesale, I suppose?" he asked thoughtfully.

"Aye, that's right. All perfectly legal."

"Oh, I don't doubt it. But if you don't mind my saying so, you seem to have rather a lot of it."

Me Winter gave him a look reserved for idiots of the first order. "You call this a lot?" he said. "This is nothing. And, in any case, as you may have noticed, it's a verra big garden."

Seventeen

With their first round of interviews complete, Spence and Laurel decided to leave Marlby Manor for the moment and continue their enquiries elsewhere.

Fortunately, Spence had taken the precaution of parking his Ford Granada in a patch of shade, so the car was relatively habitable when they returned to it.

"Where to now?" asked Laurel.

"I think well go and see the Bannerman family," said Spence thoughtfully. "I've got all the family addresses from Miss Green. The Bannerman's are over at Hattley."

"Let me see — the Bannerman's are Lady Dinnister's son-in-law Edward and her grandson Alec, aren't they?"

"Yes, that's right."

"Do you think they'll be in this afternoon?"

"I don't know," said Spence, "but it's worth a try. They probably realise that we'll want to see them at some time or other, but I prefer not to give them too much warning. We'll go and see, anyway."

They drove in silence for a mile or so, down narrow, leafy lanes with healthy-looking fields of corn on either side.

"You know," said Laurel eventually, "finding all that arsenic in the gardener's shed worried me a bit. It's disturbing to find so much of that stuff just lying around where anyone could get at it."

"I agree with you to some extent," said Spence, "but not entirely. You see, if you really want to kill someone, you can do it with a carving knife or any other household implement, so the availability of a poison is not all that worrying in itself. And I should imagine that old Me Winter handles it as responsibly as anyone. And then another factor, of course, is that we don't really know that that was the source of the arsenic that killed Miss Fosdyke."

"No," Laurel admitted, "but I bet it was. And if it was, that narrows down the field of suspects a bit — to those who either lived in the house or had regular access to it."

"Which is more or less as usual," said Spence with a rueful grin. "In any murder case, you always look to the victim's nearest and dearest for your chief suspects."

"What do you make of the people we've seen so far?" asked Laurel.

"What do you make of them?" Spence replied, throwing the question back and keeping his eyes on the road as he drove.

"Well — " Laurel paused. "Before I answer that, let's think about one or two other things. First of all, the availability of the murder weapon, or in this case the poison. Now, we've already established that there was a source of arsenic close at hand, so that's no problem. Everyone had access to that. And secondly, the opportunity to commit the murder. Well, again, that's fairly straightforward. Any one of our suspects could have just waited until Mr. Winter's back was turned and then taken a pinch or two of arsenic, mixed it with some sherry, and delivered it to the house by post, or left it on the doorstep or something like that. And then there's motive. Which in this case is simple. They all seem to be going to inherit some of Lady Dinnister's money. The secretary is hoping to get married, so she could do with it to buy a house. The butler no doubt needs a little nest egg for his old age, and Hazel and the chauffeur need capital for this restaurant they're hoping to buy."

"And those are strong enough motives for murder, are they?" asked Spence with a surprisingly cheerful smile.

"Well, on the face of it, no," Laurel admitted. "I wouldn't normally think so. The people I've mentioned are just like you and me; they could do with a bit more cash at the end of the week. But it's a funny thing about money. I always remember a few years ago, when my wife was still alive and I was earning even less than I am now. We were waiting for a big pay raise, and the negotiations were going on and on, and inflation was going up and up and up. I was using a credit card and not telling my wife, and getting deeper and deeper into debt. And then one day I went outside, and it seemed that every kid in the entire street had a new bike except mine! And for about five minutes I became absolutely incensed at the injustice of it all. All these bloody salesmen and teachers could apparently afford bicycles for their children, and I couldn't. And in that five minutes I could cheerfully have committed any crime in the book, and I wouldn't have felt it was wrong at all."

"Ah yes, but that's just the point," Spence told him. "You were tempted, but you *didn't* commit a crime. And that's the crucial difference between an honest man and a thief or a murderer. We all get angry and resentful and jealous at times, but we don't all let it get the better of us. So what we're looking for is a man whose greed or anger outweighs his sense of right and wrong to the point where he can commit murder and feel fully justified in doing so."

"Could be a woman," Laurel reminded him.

"Yes," Spence acknowledged. "It could be a woman."

*

On arrival at the Bannermans' Victorian house in Hattley, Spence mounted the steps to the front door and rang the bell.

After some delay Edward Bannerman answered the ring, and Spence introduced himself and his colleague and explained why they had called.

"Oh yes, of course," said Edward. "A nasty business, Miss Fosdyke dying like that. Lady Dinnister gave me a ring earlier on and told me all about it, so I've been sort of expecting someone to drop by. You'd better come in."

Spence and Laurel accepted the invitation and entered the spacious hall. As they did so, Spence noticed that Edward had a piece of rag in his hand that was stained all colours of the rainbow.

"Were you doing some painting?" he asked.

"Yes, I was, as a matter of fact."

"Well, then, perhaps we could talk in your studio? I'd be interested to see how it's set up."

Edward seemed slightly surprised by this request. "Well, yes, certainly, if that's what you'd like. I was just cleaning up, as it happens. I've had enough for one day."

Edward Bannerman led the way down a passage to what was obviously a specially built extension at the back of the house, a capacious artist's studio with ample light flooding in through the glass roof. The floor of the studio was cluttered but not untidy; everything clearly had its place. On an easel in the centre of the room was a picture in progress, a slightly idealised landscape in the Constable tradition, with thatched roofs, green fields, and a mountain of clouds in the sky.

"Shan't keep you a minute," said Edward. "I'm just cleaning my brushes and palette."

"That's all right," said Spence. "I don't mind having a look round."

As Edward worked, Spence pottered about the studio, picking up a canvas here and a print there, and generally displaying what was in fact a genuine interest in the artist's work. In addition to looking at the pictures, Spence also spent some time examining Edward Bannerman himself. He was about fifty-five, Spence decided. Above the waist he was a heavily built man with the torso of a wrestler or a weightlifter, but there was no sign of a beer belly lower down. He had spiky black hair, cut short, with patches of grey in it, and clear, keen eyes, which moved rapidly as he worked. His clothes were casual and paint-stained but had evidently been of excellent quality when originally purchased; he wore a cream shirt, open at the neck, with the sleeves rolled up, a pair of dark brown slacks held up by a belt, and sandals. If anything, Spence thought, he looked more like an engineer than an artist.

"Tell me about this studio," said Spence. "Did you have it specially built?"

"Yes, I did. A good many years ago now. There was a period in my life when I was briefly fashionable, believe it or not. Being the son-in-law of Lady Dinnister did no harm — she had some very useful contacts in the art world. Anyway, for a while there I made quite a lot of money, and I was sensible enough to invest some of it in plant."

"I remember seeing some of your work about ten years ago," said Spence. "You had an exhibition in Downsea." Edward looked up in surprise. "Oh — you saw that, did you?"

"Yes. I liked it very much. In fact, I wanted to buy one of your pictures, but it had been sold already."

"Oh." Edward clearly didn't quite know whether to believe that or not. "You're not much of a modernist, then?"

"No. I like my pictures to be of recognisable objects." Edward chuckled. "Well, you can see what the objects in my pictures are, all right. Mostly landscapes and portraits."

"I see you've painted a copy of Millais's *Blind Girl*," said Spence.

"Yes. I was commissioned to do that, of course, by a rather sentimental old lady. That's what buys the groceries, you know, that sort of thing. Copies of famous pictures and landscapes for Christmas cards — portraits when anybody orders one. If you're sensible, and charge by the hour for your time and cover the cost of materials, then you can make a fairly reasonable living as an artist. But, of course, I'm not so much an artist as an illustrator. I haven't any real talent, you see. Just a certain technical facility."

"Oh, I wouldn't say that," said Spence.

"And I teach a bit as well, of course. I enjoy that." Edward finished his cleaning operations and put down his piece of rag. "Well, interesting though this conversation is, you didn't come here to talk about art."

"No," Spence admitted, "we didn't. Is your son in?"

"Yes, he's upstairs."

"Would you ask him to join us, please?"

"Of course."

Edward moved off to find his son Alec, and a few minutes later the four men were sitting comfortably in easy chairs in the living room. Edward lit a cigar. "Well now," he said, blowing out the match, "is it really true that someone tried to poison my mother-in-law, and that old Fosdyke copped it instead?"

"It looks that way," said Spence cautiously.

"Oh." Edward scratched the back of his neck. "Well, I must say I find that a bit hard to believe. Why should anyone want to kill Lady Dinnister?"

"That's what I want to ask you," said Spence. "How do you get on with her yourself, for instance?"

Edward blinked a bit but answered promptly. "Well, you certainly believe in getting straight to the point, don't you? But, since you ask, I get on very well with her, thank you very much. I've certainly never had any of the traditional mother-in-law problems, and I think most of the credit for that goes to her. I was never any great catch for her daughter; in fact, in many ways I was obviously a bit of a liability. But when my late wife and I decided we wanted to get married, it was just accepted, and that was that. In fact, I was warmly welcomed into the family circle."

"Were you working as an artist in those days?"

"Trying to, yes. My family owned a small provincial newspaper, and they did their best to get me interested in running it. But it was no use; I was an absolute failure at business, so they just let me get on with painting pictures instead."

Spence turned to Lady Dinnister's grandson. "What about you, Alec; what sort of a relationship do you have with Lady Dinnister?"

119

Alec Bannerman's expression indicated that he was obviously much more resentful of this line of questioning than his father, but he too answered readily. "A very good one, I should say."

"You've had no rows with her?"

"No."

"She doesn't disapprove of your dress, or your tastes in music, or your choice of girlfriends?"

"Well, obviously we don't always see eye to eye on everything. We're of different generations. But when we do have differences of opinion, she usually makes a joke of it."

"I see. So you both get on well with her?"

Edward nodded. "Yes."

"However," said Spence, "leaving aside all personal antagonisms, we don't have to look far for a motive, do we?"

"You mean," said Edward, "a motive for my son and myself to wish to see Lady Dinnister dead?"

"Yes."

Edward sighed. "Well, that's a pretty insulting question, in a way, but I suppose it's your job to ask it. And I imagine you're talking about the money?"

"Yes."

Edward paused for a moment. His face looked sad. "Ah yes, indeed. The money. Well, I suppose there are still a few people around who think it solves problems."

"Yes. Your daughter, for instance, and her husband."

That was a bit too much, even for Edward Bannerman's mild temperament. He grew visibly angry and drew fiercely on his cigar before commenting. "You seem remarkably well informed," he said tartly.

"Murder is a serious business," Spence reminded him.

Edward thought about that for a second and then relaxed. "Well, yes, I must admit that you're right. And I suppose you know about the proposal to sell the house then, do you?"

"You mean Marlby Manor?"

"Yes."

"Tell me anyway."

Edward tapped the ash off his cigar into a brass tray. He seemed very unhappy but in control of himself. "Well, it's come up before, and I dare say it will come up again. The basic fact of the matter is that my daughter and her husband both feel that Lady Dinnister should sell Marlby Manor and move to somewhere more modest, where she would have less worry and less of a drain on her finances."

"That seems sensible enough."

"Yes, well, they also feel it would be sensible for Lady Dinnister to transfer the proceeds of the sale to the beneficiaries of her will, in order to minimize capital transfer tax when she eventually does die. That is also, in theory, quite sensible. It may be tactless and unkind to talk to an old lady about death duties, but that's a separate issue."

"So you've discussed all that as a family?"

"Yes. Quite recently."

"And you put it to Lady Dinnister?"

"Yes. I was asked to act as spokesman."

Spence turned to Alec Bannerman. "And what about you, young man — were you in favour of this proposal?"

Alec pursed his lips. "Reluctantly, yes. It was all very logical and sensible but, unfortunately, it made my sister and me look rather greedy."

"I see. And what was Lady Dinnister's response?"

Edward answered. "Well, at first she said she'd think about it. And then later she told Vernon — that's my son-in-law — that it wasn't on at all. She wasn't prepared to do it."

"And so, as things stand, if Lady Dinnister dies, who inherits her wealth?"

"Well," said Edward slowly, "on the understanding that the information is confidential, of course, I'm prepared to tell you that my two children are the main beneficiaries. I'm an executor of the will, and although I don't need to know the details of what's in it, in fact I do. And apart from the bequests to Alec and Elizabeth, there also very generous settlements to the servants."

"Almost ... excessively generous, you might say?"

"Yes. Yes, I think I would. But then, Lady Dinnister is a very generous woman — always has been."

"And she can afford to make those bequests to the servants without seriously diminishing what she will leave to your children?"

"Oh yes. She's a very wealthy woman."

Spence turned back to Alec again. "I believe you've been working on a farm this summer."

Alec sat up a bit straighten "Yes. Yes, I have. Why do you ask?"

"Oh — just interested. What kind of farm is it?"

"A dairy farm, chiefly."

"So there are lots of cows."

"Yes."

"Any sheep?"

"No — none at all."

"And you're not working there any longer?"

"No."

"Why not?"

"Well, I've got some studying to do for the next couple of weeks or so. After that I want to have a holiday before term starts."

"I see." Spence nodded. "Tell me, Alec, how did you get on with Miss Fosdyke?"

Alec glanced at his father, as if seeking permission to reply, but Edward chewed his cigar and made no response. "Well — all right, I suppose."

"How did she feel about your relationship with Susan Green?"

"I've no idea." Alec seemed quite astounded that Spence should ask such a thing.

"She never said?"

"No. And I certainly didn't ask her. It was none of her damned business."

"What was Miss Fosdyke's attitude toward the proposal to sell Marlby Manor?"

This was an open question, but Edward replied. "She was against it."

"Why?"

"Well, I believe she took the view, which is undeniably true, that Lady Dinnister loves Marlby Manor very dearly. It's her home, she can afford to run it, so she should keep it. I think that was the way Miss Fosdyke saw it."

"I see," said Spence again. "Well, thank you. That's very interesting. Very interesting indeed."

Eighteen

"It's crazy," said Elizabeth Hassett bitterly. "It's absolutely and completely crazy." She inhaled heavily on her third cigarette of the interview and stamped around the living room, made restless by anger and frustration.

"Now don't get upset, dear," said her husband warily. He was clearly embarrassed by the depth of feeling that Elizabeth was revealing.

Spence sat back and let them fight it out between them. He was always pleased when those he was interviewing betrayed some degree of emotion; it meant that the truth was all the more likely to emerge.

"That's all very well for you to say," Elizabeth almost snarled at her husband. "'Don't get upset, darling.' But I still think she's absolutely out of her mind."

After leaving Edward Bannerman and his son, Spence and Laurel had driven on to a village called Foxford. There, after some searching, they had found Meadow View, the expensive, relatively new house owned by Vernon and Elizabeth Hassett. Vernon had returned home from work at almost the same time as Spence and Laurel had arrived, and he and his wife had "naturally" agreed to do all they could to help with Spence's enquiries.

As Elizabeth stalked about her living room, fuming with anger at the obstinacy of her grandmother, Spence sat back and examined both Elizabeth and her home.

Elizabeth was in her mid-twenties, not very tall yet slim in build; clearly, putting on weight was not a problem for her. She was dark, with black hair that had been skilfully cut, dark brown eyes, and a tanned face. Even when casually dressed, as now, her clothes were stylish and expensive. She wore a red-striped silk shirt over a pair of tight black jeans that had obviously come from some very exclusive boutique. A white silk scarf was knotted around her neck, and she was sporting four rings, a gold bracelet, and deep red nail varnish. When they had shaken hands, Spence had looked into her eyes and noticed that she was wearing contact lenses; she had also applied liberal doses of a powerful and exotic perfume.

Meadow View was furnished along much the same lines as Elizabeth was dressed. The living room looked as if it had just been prepared to be photographed for *Homes and Gardens*. Among the host of items of furniture and decoration, Spence noticed a Persian carpet, Sanderson wallpaper, and some Waterford glass. The whole atmosphere was in marked contrast to the relaxed untidiness of the Bannerman household that Spence and Laurel had just left.

Elizabeth continued her tirade against Lady Dinnister. She shrugged, as if disclaiming all further responsibility for the matter. "Oh well, we've done our best to get her to see sense. And if she's too old and too stubborn to see what's best for her, then that's her problem." She sat down, still inhaling furiously on her cigarette.

Vernon Hassett had a hunted look about him; he was clearly very apprehensive about what his wife would say next, and as a result Spence decided to develop the line of questioning which had led to Elizabeth's outburst.

"So," he said, "the position as I understand it is this: you and your husband and your brother and your father — you all agree that Marlby Manor should be sold."

Vernon Hassett leapt in while his wife was still inhaling cigarette smoke. "Yes, that's right, Superintendent. We take the view that Marlby Manor is too big and too expensive for Lady Dinnister to run at this stage of her life. All right, granted she's very wealthy and can afford it in principle. And granted that she has a sentimental attachment to the place. We know all that. But even so, running a household as large as the manor imposes a very considerable strain. She has all the problems of finding staff and keeping them, of maintaining the place, insuring it, looking after the grounds, and so on. It's our view that she would be far better off selling the manor and moving to somewhere smaller. And as her adviser, I've told her so."

Spence almost smiled. "You regard yourself as one of her advisers, do you?" he asked politely.

Vernon Hassett detected no hint of sarcasm or doubt in Spence's tone. "Yes, frankly, I do. She has bankers and lawyers and so forth, but in terms of family I think I can say, without blowing my own trumpet, that I'm the only one with any experience of business. Her son-in-law, Elizabeth's father, well, he's an absolutely charming man, but by his own admission he's got no judgement in financial matters at all. And Alec, of course, is too young."

"Yes," said Spence, "I see. And what sort of work do you do, Mr. Hassett?"

Vernon pushed his glasses further back on his nose. "I'm an executive with Wallace's," he said. "I'm in marketing, actually." He certainly looked like an eager young executive, with his fashionably cut, grey lightweight suit, black shoes, blue tie, and hair so immaculately arranged that Spence suspected it had been both permed and lacquered.

"Wallace's," Spence repeated. "That's a food-canning firm isn't it?"

"Yes."

"I see. Have you been with them long?"

"Ten years."

"Ever since you left school, in fact?"

Vernon nodded. He hadn't liked that bit about "ever since leaving school"; he preferred people to think that he'd been to a university.

"Do you have a job, Mrs. Hassett?" asked Spence.

"Me?" said Elizabeth in surprise. "No — no, not at the moment. We're thinking of starting a boutique, as a matter of fact, but it's still at the planning stage."

"Do you have some experience in that line of business?"

"I took a degree in design," said Elizabeth shortly. "I like to think that my knowledge of fashion is as extensive as anyone's." She stubbed out her cigarette and immediately reached for another one.

"Do you think there would be any difficulty in selling Marlby Manor?" asked Spence. "I must say I wouldn't care to take it on myself."

Vernon shook his head firmly. "No, no trouble at all, Superintendent. As a matter of fact, we've had several informal approaches already. It's the kind of place that appeals to the Arabs, you know. Secluded, private, plenty of scope for development, nice grounds — there's even room for an airstrip."

"What sort of price would it fetch?"

"Half a million pounds minimum. Maybe three-quarters. The market is going up all the time."

"And if," said Spence, "if the manor were sold, then presumably Lady Dinnister would be in a position to pass on most of that capital sum to her grandchildren?"

"Exactly." Vernon nodded eagerly, apparently delighted to have found someone who followed his own line of reasoning. "You've put your finger right on it. Lady Dinnister admits herself that one of her major objectives is to leave as much money as she can to her heirs, and by passing on the proceeds of the sale now, she could reduce capital transfer tax very considerably."

"But," Spence continued, "the fact remains that Lady Dinnister has not agreed to this scheme."

"No, not at the moment. Not yet." Vernon opened his hands. "But — we'll have another go at her later."

"Tell me, how did Lady Dinnister's staff feel about this idea of yours?"

Vernon looked blank. "I've no idea."

"They were dead against it, obviously," said Elizabeth.

"Why?"

"Well, because they'd lose their jobs. They've got a very nice cushy number at the moment. They've got nothing to do, and they're very well paid for it. All they have to do is say, 'Yes, Lady Dinnister; no, Lady Dinnister; thank you very much, Lady Dinnister' — so naturally they would oppose any change as hard as they could."

"And what did Miss Fosdyke think about it?"

"Oh!" Elizabeth almost shouted. "She was the worst of the lot. At least she's out of the way; that's one blessed relief."

Vernon looked severely embarrassed once again. "We mustn't speak ill of the dead, darling," he suggested.

"I don't see why not. She never spoke well of me when she was alive. Miserable old bitch."

"You didn't see eye to eye then?" Spence suggested mildly.

"No, we did not. I thought she was a nosy, prying old maid, and I told her so. She was a servant, just like the rest of them — a paid companion — but she acted like she was the Queen Mother or something."

There was silence after that. Elizabeth seemed to have run out of steam at last, and Vernon was too embarrassed to say anything.

After a moment Spence decided to bring the interview to an end. He stood up to go, and Laurel, taking his cue, folded up his notebook.

Spence advanced to the large double-glazed window which opened onto the extensive garden at the back of the house. "Are you a keen gardener, Mr. Hassett?" he asked.

"No, not very." Vernon Hassett joined him at the window. "Why do you ask?"

"Oh, because it all seems so beautifully kept. I can't see a weed anywhere."

"Oh well," said Vernon, "we have a man who comes in to do most of that. I can't claim much credit, I'm afraid."

Spence turned to look back at Elizabeth, who was still sitting in her chair, looking thoroughly disgruntled. "What about you, Mrs. Hassett. Have you got green fingers?"

"Me?" echoed Elizabeth. "No, I'm no gardener. As my grandmother is always telling me, I can't tell a lettuce from a lupin."

"Oh dear," said Spence. "Well, in that case, Mrs. Hassett, I would advise you to be extremely careful. Should you ever be rash enough to eat one, you would find that lupins are poisonous."

Nineteen

"How do you know?" Laurel asked suddenly.

"How do I know what?" said Spence, who was driving the pair of them back to the police house at Marlby.

"How do you know that lupins are poisonous?"

Spence laughed as he changed gear on the narrow, winding road. "Oh, because of my attempts at making wine out of elderflowers and things like that. I came across a list of poisonous plants in a book somewhere. It turns out that a surprising number of flowers are poisonous — bluebells, buttercups, and daffodils, for a start. Dandelions, elderberries, and parsnips, on the other hand, are all pretty good; you can make excellent wine out of them. If you know how."

Laurel was unconvinced. "Hmm, well, I'd rather you drank it than me … Anyway, what about this young fellow Hassett? He went on and on about how Lady Dinnister should sell the manor, and his wife went on and on about what a miserable old bag Lady Dinnister was because she wouldn't sell. Do you think they realise that all they're doing is explaining what an excellent motive they have for trying to get rid of her?"

Spence grinned. "I doubt it. I don't think they're bright enough, either of them. But it could be all an elaborate double bluff. Very often people lie in order to avoid bringing suspicion on themselves, and we've probably got a few people doing that in this case. But, occasionally, people try to deceive us in a different way. They make a point of seeming to be transparently honest and sincere in their efforts to help, so that however strong a motive they have, we end up feeling that they're too naive and unworldly to be involved in anything so ruthless as murder. And this one is a very deliberate case of murder; let's not have any doubt about that."

"I wonder what Vernon Hassett's income is?" Laurel pondered aloud.

"I don't know, but I think you'd better find out. I shall be surprised if his salary is any higher than mine, and I certainly couldn't live in a style like that. Lady Dinnister told us that they were an extravagant young couple, and I should imagine they're up to their eyes in debt."

"Yes," said Laurel, "I'll make a few enquiries. See if he's finished paying for all that carpet, for instance."

"And while you're at it," said Spence, "run a check on Edward Bannerman's credit-worthiness, too. He claims to be making a living out of his paintbrush, but just see if it's true." A few minutes later the two men arrived back at the police house in Marlby, where they had established their headquarters earlier in the day. Detective Sergeant Wilberforce, as expected, was still on duty, and documents for Spence's attention were neatly laid out in a pile, the edges of the reports absolutely in line with the edge of the table that supported them.

The most interesting of the papers was the account of Dr. Dunbar's postmortem examination of Miss Fosdyke. Spence read it through carefully, initialled it, and passed it on to Laurel. Another useful document for reference was a copy of the initial report to the chief constable and others, which Spence had dictated at lunchtime. After Laurel had read both of these, Spence retrieved them and stuck them in his briefcase.

"Well," said Laurel, "what do we do now?"

"What we do now," said Spence, "is make a list of the names of all the people we've come across today and arrange to have them checked against criminal records."

"I've done that," said Laurel. "I did it while you were reading the p.m. report."

"Oh. Good. What about arranging for a patrol car to keep a special eye on Marlby Manor tonight? I suppose we ought to be thinking about the possibility of someone trying a second attack on Lady Dinnister, although I'm bound to say I think it's pretty unlikely."

"That's done, too," said Laurel.

"Oh. Well, in that case we'll go home."

Laurel seemed distinctly surprised.

"Unless, of course," Spence continued, "you can think of anything else to do?"

"No, no, not at all," said Laurel hastily. "As a matter of fact, I've got a date tonight, so I shall be quite glad to get away. I thought I was going to have to cancel it."

"Oh?" said Spence with interest. "Anyone I know?" Laurel looked a little sheepish. "Well, um, yes. As it happens, I'm going out with Patricia North — I met her at the party at your place last Friday."

"Oh yes," said Spence, trying hard to keep a straight face. "Yes, well, she's a very nice person, is Patricia — I'm sure you'll enjoy yourself. Just make sure you're back here promptly tomorrow morning, that's all. Eight-thirty sharp, please."

*

Half an hour later, at seven o'clock, Spence arrived at his home, which was a detached three-bedroom house on the north side of Wellbridge. He discovered that his wife Julia had abandoned all hope of his returning at any reasonable hour and had not given any thought to an evening meal.

"Never mind," said Spence. "It's too hot to eat much anyway. How about a sandwich?"

"Chicken suit you?" asked Julia.

"Yes. That will do very nicely."

While Julia prepared his sandwich, Spence opened a bottle of Graves with a loud pop.

"What's this for?" asked Julia. "Not a celebration, surely? You haven't solved this case already?"

"No," Spence admitted, "I can't say I have. But I thought we ought to drink a little toast. Guess which widow is going out with which widower tonight?"

Julia stopped buttering bread for a moment and stood up straight, her eyes gleaming. "Not Patricia North and your Mr. Laurel?"

"None other," said Spence gleefully. "The very same."

Julia resumed her task, looking very pleased with herself. "Well, that is good news. It didn't take very long, did it? Lucky you managed to finish work in reasonable time tonight."

"Yes," said Spence, "otherwise poor Patricia might have been given quite the wrong impression about police work. She might have got the idea that we keep men out late at night."

"Now, now," said Julia as she carried her husband's sandwich into the living room. "There's no need to be sarcastic about it. Anyway, I'm awfully glad they're going out together; your Mr. Laurel has the rumpled and dishevelled air of a man in need of a good woman."

Spence put his feet up while he ate his supper and drank half the bottle of Graves; Julia sipped at the other half. As she did so, she read through the documents about the Fosdyke murder case that Spence had brought home in his briefcase.

At thirty-four, Julia Spence was five years younger than her husband. She was an attractive, healthy-looking woman with a full, rounded figure and shoulder-length brown hair. By profession, Julia was a lecturer in psychology at the South-shire College of Higher Education and, whenever possible, Spence liked to discuss his cases with her. He found that very often she was able to suggest fresh lines of approach, particularly when he himself was feeling stale and had run out of ideas.

After he had finished eating, Spence dictated some notes on the afternoon's interviews into his pocket tape recorder while Julia listened. When he had finished, Julia went off to make them some coffee and then returned.

"Well," said Spence, "now that you've read the documents and listened to my account of the interviews, you know very nearly as much about this case as I do. So who's the guilty party?"

Julia stirred her coffee thoughtfully. "You say there are about five deaths a year from arsenic poisoning?"

"Five *known* deaths."

"Hmm. And the stuff is readily available to anyone with a bit of initiative — certainly easily available in this case because there's a can of it in Mr. McWinter's woodshed."

"And, possibly, on the farm where Alec Bannerman was working. And probably elsewhere, too."

"Yes. I wonder if artists use arsenic for anything?"

"I don't know, but we can find out."

"In any case," Julia continued, "the fact is that although the sale of arsenic is much more tightly controlled now than it used to be, there really isn't much problem about getting hold of it if you want to kill someone."

"Precisely."

"All right. And then we come to the way in which it was administered. That doesn't require any special skill either, as far as I can see. You just open a bottle of sherry, dissolve some arsenic in water, presumably, tip it into the bottle, and reseal it with one of those plastic tops that you seal your homemade wine bottles with."

"Dead easy," said Spence.

"And you think it was only by chance that Miss Fosdyke opened the sherry instead of Lady Dinnister?"

"Well, yes."

"What do you mean, 'Well, yes'?"

"What I mean," said Spence, "is that that's what worries me. You see, it's not a very specific murder weapon. It's not like stabbing somebody, where you can see exactly who it is you're trying to kill. If the compliments card that we found with the bottle of sherry means what we think it does, then the wrong person died — and that's not very efficient murdering. And even if we suppose that Lady Dinnister *had* opened the bottle, she could have served the sherry to anyone and given herself gin-and-tonic instead. So that's what worries me — that someone went to a great deal of trouble to manufacture a murder weapon that both could, and apparently did, hit the wrong target."

"But perhaps there was only enough arsenic in it to kill a weak old woman. Perhaps other people would just have been sick."

"Well, perhaps so," said Spence. "We shall know tomorrow morning anyway; it was being analysed this afternoon."

"Let's move on to the motive," said Julia. "That's what interests me. If I can wear my academic hat for a minute, it seems to me as a psychologist that the driving force of nearly all human activity is control of the environment. In other words, men seek to control the environment in order to be able to mate — even if they're past the age of mating. And women seek to control the environment in order to bring up their children safely."

"They're seeking security," said Spence.

"Yes. Now, that in itself is not very illuminating, of course, until it's expressed in more concrete terms. So we ask ourselves, what constitutes the means of controlling the environment here? And in this case the concrete term seems to be money."

"Indeed it does," said Spence.

"Now there's a further aspect to this desire for money that I think you ought to consider. The desire itself has to be there, of course — and it's present in most of us to some degree. But, in order to justify murder, the desire for money has to be present in tremendous intensity. And the same is true of any other motive, such as revenge. We all feel the urge to get our own back occasionally, but we don't all feel it with such overwhelming strength that we go out and kill someone. And the only way you're ever going to be able to judge whether or not that level of intensity exists in your suspects is by knowing a very great deal about their backgrounds — about their hopes and secret longings. In short, about what makes them tick."

"So what you're saying," said Spence slowly, "is that what I ought to be trying to find out in this case is which one of these people is really absolutely desperate enough to kill?"

"I would say so, yes."

"Which doesn't necessarily mean just the one with the least money."

"Unfortunately, no. You see, another point about motive is that the consequences of *not* murdering must seem far worse than the risks involved in actually committing the crime. Take this young couple, the Hassetts, for example. Now, I'm not saying that they're the guilty parties, but just suppose they were on the brink of some terrible financial disaster. Bankruptcy, having their house repossessed by the building society, or something like that. To a very status-conscious young couple, that might seem absolutely intolerable."

"It would seem pretty appalling to me," said Spence with a grin.

"A couple like that, very keen on keeping up with the Joneses, might very easily be provoked into crime, despite the fact that on the face of it they're pretty well off … And another factor you ought to look at is the temperamental ability to kill."

"Yes," said Spence. "Susan Green mentioned that earlier on today. The killer instinct, you mean — the thing boxers are supposed to have."

"Well, almost. I was thinking more of people who are used to taking life in one form or another. Butchers, farmers, soldiers, and doctors. Those sorts of people."

"Doctors don't take life," said Spence argumentatively.

"Well, not usually, no. But they can look death in the eye and keep a very steady hand."

"There is a doctor in this case, of course," said Spence thoughtfully. "Dr. Milton. He'd have access to arsenic, I suppose. And he's also been left some money in Lady Dinnister's will."

"You'd better add him to the list of suspects, then."

"Yes, I suppose so."

"And what about the Karpman triangle?" suggested Julia.

"The what?"

"The Karpman triangle."

"What about it?" said Spence. "I might be able to give you a better answer if I knew what it was myself."

Julia laughed. "Well, it's a sort of framework of relationships drawn up by a man called Karpman. And the idea is that in every situation involving conflict, or potential conflict, you have a victim, a rescuer, and a persecutor."

"And how does that help me in this case?" asked Spence, who was sometimes less than captivated by his wife's psychological jargon.

"Well, it sometimes helps to shed a bit of light on a situation," Julia continued. "For instance, Lady Dinnister is apparently a victim — or at any rate an intended victim. But the reason she is a victim is because to someone else she appears to be a persecutor. And perhaps she appears to be a persecutor to that person because she is acting as a rescuer to someone else."

Spence shook his head. "You've lost me, I'm afraid."

"Well, take a concrete example. Lady Dinnister altered her will in favour of her grandchildren, to exclude Edward Bannerman. So she is a rescuer to them. But, conversely, as far as Edward Bannerman was concerned, she might have been a persecutor. Perhaps he had dreams of going off to Tahiti like Gauguin."

Spence was doubtful. "Hmmm, yes, maybe. I'll give it some thought. But with the greatest respect to your Mr. Karpman, his triangle seems to be a good deal more useful to him than it is to me." He put his hands behind his head and yawned.

Julia smiled. "Well, keep the idea in mind. You never know when it might prove helpful." She glanced at the clock and changed the subject. "I wonder where Patricia North and your Mr. Laurel have got to. Were they going out to dinner, do you think?"

"Something like that," said Spence.

"I wonder what they're talking about."

Spence chuckled. "Hah! Probably wondering what the hell to say to each other. Wondering how on earth they ever let the Spences get them into such a mess."

"Oh, come now," said Julia reproachfully. "It won't be as bad as all that, surely. They're very well suited to each other."

"Well, let's hope so," said Spence. "Otherwise I'm not going to be a very popular man first thing tomorrow morning."

Twenty

Spence was awake very early the next morning. He lay in bed, listening to the extraordinary din made by the birds in the garden, and thinking back over the events of the previous day.

There was something about a poisoning that made him very angry indeed. It was a cowardly, deliberately wicked sort of crime, with particularly unpleasant consequences for the wretched victim. A stabbing, or a strangling, or a heavy blow with the fist — all of those were violent responses to stress and conflict that Spence could understand, and to some degree forgive; but the cold, premeditated administration of poison was something else again. He was determined to get to the bottom of this case, and preferably before the day was out.

Spence got up soon after six, showered, dressed, and cooked himself his usual formidable breakfast. Then he went upstairs to say good-bye to Julia, who was just beginning to stir.

"Going already?" she murmured, turning over at his kiss on her cheek.

"Yes, I'm afraid so."

"Ben ... "

"Yes?"

Julia sat up in bed and hugged her knees. "I hardly dare ask, but is there any chance that we shall be able to start our holiday on Saturday, as planned?"

Spence grinned ruefully. "Your guess is as good as mine," he said.

Spence drove first to Wellbridge Police Headquarters, where he collected a number of reports and letters. Then he drove on to the police house at Marlby. pausing only to buy a selection of morning newspapers en route.

It was a quarter to eight when he arrived at Marlby, which gave him just enough time to read through the paperwork before Detective Sergeant Wilberforce arrived at eight-fifteen. Laurel arrived five minutes later, looking distinctly bleary-eyed.

Spence handed Wilberforce the tape he had dictated the previous evening, with instructions to get it typed. Then he saw to it that

Wilberforce provided the three of them with large cups of coffee, and finally they all sat down around a table for a briefing.

"Right," said Spence briskly, rubbing his hands together. "Let's get on. First of all. I'll bring you up to date on this morning's mail; there's some quite interesting stuff come in. Number one, all the names we submitted to criminal records have got a negative response — so there are no hardened criminals among the people we've met so far. Number two. Lady Dinnister's hair dryer was not deliberately tampered with. The reason it gave Hazel a nasty shock was that it was just too old to be safe any longer. Another of the so-called attempts on Lady Dinnister's life can also be ruled out. The owner of the garage where she gets her Rolls-Royce serviced has admitted, when pressed, that he did not double-check that her wheel was put back on properly. On the contrary, he didn't check it at all, and there have been other instances of similar carelessness on the part of his mechanics."

"What about the other accident Lady Dinnister mentioned?" asked Laurel. "The flowers that nearly gave her lockjaw or anthrax or something."

"Also slipshod work. I don't know what the hell the world's coming to these days: no one seems to do their job properly. Anyway, the fact of the matter is that the florist who sent the flowers has had other complaints about the way bouquets have been fastened together with any old bits of rusty wire, and she is taking steps to reprimand the staff involved, etcetera, etcetera."

"So, in other words, there weren't any three previous attempts to kill Lady Dinnister at all?" suggested Laurel.

"Exactly." Spence turned over the report from the officer who had questioned the florist and went on to the next sheet of paper. "Now then, progress at last — news from Forensic. They confirm, as we assumed, that arsenic is present in the sherry bottle in quite lethal proportions. They have also examined the ribbon that we took off Susan Green's typewriter and have discovered — surprise, surprise — that the compliments slip that was supposed to come from Williams and Williams, wine merchants of High Street, Wellbridge, was in fact typed on that machine. But on a different head from the two that Susan Green uses."

"Ah," said Laurel, sitting back in his chair. "Now that is interesting. Surely what that means is that it was typed by someone living in the house. Someone bright enough to realise that it would look a bit odd if a Williams and Williams compliments slip were typed in the same style as Susan Green's letters and so forth, but not bright enough to realise that it would show up on the ribbon."

"Or," said Spence, "being devious for a moment, it might have been done by someone with access to the house, who wanted us to *think* that it was typed by a resident. And who wanted us to *think* that the person concerned wasn't very bright. Remember, as I keep reminding you, and myself, this was not a hasty crime of passion. It was thought about and planned, over a considerable period of time. But I'll tell you what worries me about it."

"What's that?"

"Well, if the person responsible was someone living in the house, surely they could have worked out a way to guarantee that the poison got to the right person."

Laurel thought about it. "Not easy," he said after a moment. "Not if you're going to hide behind this idea that it was a complimentary bottle. The only way to guarantee that it got to the right person would be by pouring it out yourself, and that would surely be a bit too risky."

"Yes," said Spence heavily, "I suppose you're right. And for the record, of course, that complimentary bottle business is all nonsense, too. Williams and Williams deny having sent any such bottle, and they have had no dealings with Lady Dinnister whatsoever."

"What about fingerprints on the bottle?" asked Laurel.

"Ah, that's more promising." Spence licked his fingers and drew on another report from the pile in front of him. "Three separate sets of prints have been identified. One belongs to a person unknown, and my guess is that those were put there by whoever sold it over the counter. Another set belongs to Miss Fosdyke. And the third set belongs to — guess who — Miss Susan Green."

"Mmm, interesting!" said Laurel, his eyes opening wide. "So she handled the bottle. I wonder when?"

"Me too," said Spence. "Which reminds me — do a job card to get prints taken from Edward and Alec Bannerman, the Hassetts, and Dr. Milton. Just so that we can identify or eliminate them as necessary."

Wilberforce seized a pen and scribbled out an instruction accordingly.

"Right," Spence continued. "Well, that's about it, so far." He tossed the pile of reports over to Laurel. "You'd better read through them all to see if you can spot anything new, and in the meantime I'll have a look at the morning papers."

"Right you are," said Laurel.

Wilberforce retired to his office in another room, and there was silence for the next twenty minutes while Spence read a succession of newspaper stories of the "Arsenic Kills Elderly Spinster" type. Then he went out into Wilberforce's office and gave him instructions on a couple of points that he had thought of while reading the papers.

When Laurel had finished reading the reports, Spence tossed the newspapers to one side. "Notice anything new in those reports?" he asked.

Laurel shook his head. "No. Can't say I did. I think you covered most of it in your briefing. What do you propose to do now?"

"Well, I think we'll go and see Susan Green, and ask her how her fingerprints came to be on that bottle of sherry."

"Yes, why not?" said Laurel, and the two men made for the door.

"I'll tell you one thing that's just struck me," said Spence as they walked across the garden to his car. "Do you remember reading that postmortem report op Miss Fosdyke yesterday afternoon?"

"Yes," said Laurel guardedly, wondering what he'd missed this time.

"Well, I had another look at it this morning, and there was one thing in it that Dunbar might have mentioned to us verbally, but he probably didn't think to because he knew Miss Fosdyke personally. Apparently, she had prenormal occlusion."

"Oh? What does that mean?"

"Well, it's a slight deformity of the jaw. It means that when she closed her mouth, her lower teeth met her upper teeth in front, rather than behind, as is the case in most people. It means she would have had a rather prominent jaw."

Laurel stopped in his tracks. "Oh," he said. "You mean like Len Jones?"

"Yes," said Spence with a smile. "Just like him."

Laurel frowned. "Presumably it's hereditary," he said thoughtfully. "That seems a very curious coincidence, that two people in the same household should have the same malformation of the jaw."

"Yes," said Spence. "It does seem a bit odd, doesn't it?"

Twenty-One

Mr. Tanner admitted them to Marlby Manor soon after 9:00 A.M.

"Good morning, gentlemen," he said gravely.

"Good morning," said Spence and Laurel together.

"Will you be wishing to see Lady Dinnister?"

"Not at the moment," said Spence. "I expect we'll need to see her later on, but we'd like to see Miss Green first."

"Certainly, sir," said the butler with a slight bow. "She's in her office — through there, to the left."

"Thank you very much," said Spence, and made his way across the hall to the room where he had interviewed Susan Green the day before.

The office door was half-open, and Susan had obviously overheard the conversation in the hall because she was rather flustered and nervous by the time Spence arrived.

"Oh, good morning, Superintendent," she said breathlessly, standing up and almost falling over her chair as she did so. "I was just opening the mail."

"Perhaps that could wait for a moment or two," said Spence. "We shan't keep you long."

"Yes, yes, of course."

"Please sit down again."

"Yes, thank you, I will."

Susan Green resumed her seat on the typist's chair in front of the desk, and Spence and Laurel made themselves comfortable on the two other chairs in the room. Laurel closed the door after them.

"Well now," Spence began, "let me get straight to the point. As a result of various tests, we have now established two things quite clearly. The first is that Miss Fosdyke died of arsenic poisoning, and the second is that the poison was contained in a bottle of sherry. Naturally, we have examined the bottle of sherry very carefully, and we've found three sets of fingerprints on it. Some of the fingerprints are yours, Miss Green — and we thought it only right to give you an opportunity to say how they came to be there."

Susan Green's eyes opened even wider than ever. She began to stammer. "Well, I — er — I suppose … I suppose they must have got there when I — when I poured us out some sherry."

There was a long silence, which at first Spence made no immediate attempt to fill. But eventually he said, "You poured out a glass of sherry?"

"Yes." Susan's voice was almost inaudible with nervousness.

"When?"

"Oh — er — on Monday evening."

"What time?"

"Oh — about half past six."

"Tell me about it," said Spence.

Susan drew a deep breath, obviously determined to bring herself under control. She lowered her chin, swallowed, and began to speak with more confidence.

"Well, on Monday afternoon Miss Fosdyke said she would like to have a word with me. So I said, all right, when shall we meet? And she said about half past six in her room. So I went … Well, she was very nice and polite, and she suggested we should have a glass of sherry together. And she gave me a glass."

"What about the bottle?"

"It was in a cupboard. She asked me to get it down while she was washing out a glass for herself. So I did. And then she asked me to pour."

"Was it a full bottle?"

"Yes. I had to take the top off it."

"What sort of top was it?"

"Well, some sort of plastic seal, I think. And then a cork with a round top to it — the kind of thing that you can push in and pull out again quite easily."

"I see. And then what?"

"Well, we talked."

"What about?"

"Well, about me and — Alec Bannerman."

"Ah yes, I see."

"She didn't want me to marry him, you see. At least she didn't think I should."

"Why not?"

"Well, because I'm a — little bit older than he is. And because he's ... still at university, that sort of thing. I was once stupid enough to ask her advice about whether she thought Alec was fond of me, and after that she was always going on about it."

"I see. So you sat there and drank a glass of sherry each?"

"Yes."

"And did you feel any ill effects afterwards?"

"No. None at all. I mean — should I have?"

Spence smiled. "That's not for me to say," he said. "Either you did or you didn't, and that's that."

"Well, no, I didn't feel anything wrong at all. And I never even dreamed until now — I mean I had no idea that it was the same bottle that killed her. No idea at all."

Spence seemed suddenly preoccupied and no longer very interested in Miss Green. "Well, don't worry about it; I'm sure you won't come to any harm at this stage. What did you do with the rest of the evening?"

"I — er — I went home."

"Where's that?"

"Well, I have a little cottage on the far side of the estate. It used to be let to one of the gardeners, but now that we don't have so many grounds staff, Lady Dinnister lets me live in it."

"And you didn't go out again once you got home?"

"No."

"You didn't go and see Alec Bannerman, for instance?"

"No. I rang him up."

"And did you discuss what Miss Fosdyke had said?"

"No. No, I didn't like to. I thought he would be annoyed."

"I see." Spence glanced at Laurel and then back at Susan. "I wonder if you'd mind leaving us alone for a few moments, Miss Green. My colleague and I would just like to have a discussion in private."

"Yes, yes, of course." And with almost comic haste, Susan leapt to her feet and half-ran from the room, closing the door after her.

Spence was silent for some moments, and then he sighed heavily. "Well ... " he said.

"Well, indeed," echoed Laurel. "What do you think all that means?"

Spence rubbed his forehead in an attempt to remove the worried frown that had appeared there. "Well, I'm beginning to get an inkling of what it means, and I don't much like any of it. First of all, Susan Green could be lying. It could be that she was the one who put the arsenic into the sherry and that she was in such a panic that she forgot about fingerprints."

"Yes, that's certainly a possibility," said Laurel.

"Another possibility, even more remote, is that the arsenic was in the bottle of sherry at the time when she and Miss Fosdyke drank some, and that Susan Green is immune to the stuff."

"Is that possible?" asked Laurel.

"Apparently, yes. Rasputin is alleged to have been immune to arsenic, but there's some doubt about it, and I think we can safely rule it out in this case. So that leads us to the only other explanation — "

"Which is that she's telling the truth."

"Yes. Now what are the implications of that?" Spence sat back in his chair and closed his eyes. "Do you remember the details of that forensic report on the bottle of sherry?"

"Frankly, no."

"Well I do, because they struck me at the time as being very peculiar, but in view of what Susan Green has just told us, it's beginning to make sense."

Spence reached out for a piece of paper and a pencil from the desk in front of him and began to scribble some calculations. After perhaps two minutes he nodded with satisfaction and put the pencil down.

"Right. The sums balance out. So this is how it was done." He turned to look at Laurel. "According to the forensic report, the bottle of sherry which we found in Miss Fosdyke's room contained twenty-six fluid ounces of sherry, which was twelve percent alcohol by volume, or nineteen proof. Now that bothered me a bit when I read it. You see, a full bottle of sherry would have been about twenty-eight fluid ounces, so someone had had a small drink out of it, and that makes sense because we know that Miss Fosdyke had a nightcap. But the twelve percent alcohol — that wasn't right at all. A good sherry is normally about eighteen percent alcohol by volume, and even a cheap one is fifteen percent. But if you look at these figures, you'll see what happened."

Laurel drew nearer and peered over Spence's shoulder.

"Now," Spence continued, "we start with a full bottle of good-quality sherry: twenty-eight fluid ounces and eighteen percent alcohol by volume. Miss Fosdyke and Miss Green have a small glass each. You and

I would take three or four fluid ounces in a glass, but they were rather genteel ladies, so they only had two. That leaves twenty-four ounces, still at eighteen percent alcohol. Now, along comes our murderer, later on Monday evening. He, or she, has already dissolved some arsenic in a small amount of warm water — say four fluid ounces. You wouldn't want to use much more than that or it would weaken the taste of the sherry too much. Okay so far?"

Laurel nodded.

"Good. So now you've got a full bottle again, but its alcoholic strength has been reduced by one-sixth, so it's now down to fifteen percent. So the murderer gives it a good shake to mix it all in, wearing gloves all the time, I should imagine, and then he empties out four fluid ounces to make the bottle look just as full, or as empty, as it had been before."

"And then he goes away?"

"Right. And later that night, as we know, Miss Fosdyke poured herself another little drink — say another two fluid ounces — and that is what killed her."

"But just a minute," said Laurel. "After she'd done that, the level would have gone down by about six fluid ounces. But when we found the bottle, if was almost full; there had only been about one small drink taken out of it."

"Exactly. That's what it looked like, I agree. So what does that mean?"

"Well, if you're right, it means that someone topped it up a bit, later on."

"That's right, someone did. And we know that they must have used tap water to do it. They added four fluid ounces of water, which reduced the alcoholic strength yet again, from fifteen percent to twelve. Which is why the forensic report stated that we had twenty-six fluid ounces of sherry at twelve percent alcohol by volume."

Laurel was silent for some time, thinking through the implications. Eventually Spence prompted him.

"Which means what?" he asked.

"Well," said Laurel, "it means a lot of things, some of them rather disturbing. First of all, the final topping-up must have been done on Tuesday, after Miss Fosdyke was dead."

"Correct."

"And it also means that the poison was added to a bottle which was located specifically in Miss Fosdyke's room, and at a time when it was known that the next person to have a drink from it would almost certainly be Miss Fosdyke."

"Correct again."

"But in that case, why did whoever it was bother with this card from Williams and Williams?"

"Well, I don't know for sure," said Spence, "but I can guess. First of all, the intention was to kill Miss Fosdyke, and no one else. So the murder weapon *was* aimed at a precise target, and the murderer was successful. Secondly, there was every chance that the death would be regarded as resulting from natural causes. And in many cases murder would never have been suspected. An elderly woman dying of gastroenteritis — it happens all the time. But in this case, unfortunately for our murderer, there was a postmortem, and a careful one at that, which established that arsenic was the cause of death. But that doesn't worry our murderer too much because he's got a safety device built into his plan. Once he realises that there's a risk of foul play being suspected, or even before, he does two things. First of all, he tops up the bottle, so that you and I will assume that the poison could have been put in the bottle weeks earlier, and not just in a limited period of time on Monday night. And secondly, he leaves that compliments card on the shelf beside the bottle, so that we will assume that it was really intended for Lady Dinnister."

"Both of which worked pretty well," said Laurel. "Particularly the second point. For the past twenty-four hours we've been running around trying to find motives for people wanting to kill Lady Dinnister — when what we really ought to have been looking into was who hated Miss Fosdyke."

"Yes," said Spence. "I'm afraid you're right. So we've been set back a little bit, but we've also gained some very useful ground. We know, for instance, that our circle of suspects is now limited to those who had access to Miss Fosdyke's room between, say, 7:00 P.M. and 11:00 P.M. on Monday night — and that's quite a big help."

"Yes." Now it was Laurel's turn to scribble on a piece of paper. "Let's just work out who those people are. First of all, we've got all those who live in the manor. Len Jones, Hazel Quinn, Mr. Tanner, and Lady Dinnister. And then there's another group made up of people who could walk in here without any questions being asked. Susan Green, Edward and Alec Bannerman, Mr. and Mrs. Hassett."

"And the doctor," said Spence. "You'd better include him."

"All right; Dr. Milton. And that's the lot."

"That's right. Any one of those people could easily have known about Miss Fosdyke's habit of taking a nightcap, and they could relatively easily have got into Miss Fosdyke's room for the necessary few minutes. So I think the next thing to do is to ring Mr. Wilberforce and arrange for checks to be made on those who live outside the manor. I want to know where they were from 6:30 P.M. on Monday, and all day Tuesday."

"Miss Fosdyke's room was locked for part of Tuesday," said Laurel.

"Most of Tuesday, I believe," said Spence, "but I'm not too interested in that. Anyone can get a key copied, so the murderer could have got in at almost any time."

"What about checking up on those who live in the house? Finding out where they were on Monday night."

"We'll ask them that ourselves. And we'll also ask them which of the others they saw on the premises at the appropriate time, as a cross-check."

"Hmm, okay," said Laurel. "Well, I suppose you're right; we've lost a bit of ground, and we've gained a bit too. But we're still back to square one on the question of motive. We've been looking at it from the wrong angle entirely."

"Not really," said Spence. "It's not as bad as you might think because we've collected a whole lot of information about Miss Fosdyke without quite realising it. One thing we must do, though, is this: phone the hospital and see if any of those on our list of suspects were ever referred to Miss Fosdyke in her time as an almoner there. The hospital is certain to maintain that their records are confidential and so forth, but you can deal with that, I'm sure. What I want are Miss Fosdyke's personal notes on the people involved in this case — if there are any."

Laurel reached for the phone. "Okay. I'll get onto it right now."

"And while you're doing that," said Spence, "I'll have a think about the Karpman triangle."

"The what?" said Laurel in surprise.

"The Karpman triangle. It's all a question of relationships, you see. Up to now we've been thinking of Miss Fosdyke as a victim, but in fact, in the murderer's eyes, she was a persecutor."

"Oh," said Laurel. "Really. Well, I'll leave that bit of it to you."

Spence chuckled, and Laurel began to dial.

Twenty-Two

While Laurel was on the telephone, Spence went upstairs to see Lady Dinnister. Susan Green was with her, and they had just finished discussing the contents of that day's *Financial Times*.

"You know, Mr. Spence," said Lady Dinnister as she folded up the pink newspaper and put it to one side, "a lot of people of my generation are absolutely appalled by all these strikes and so on. But I can't say they shock me very much. In a way, I can understand men going on strike very easily. Have you ever been down a coal mine?"

"No," said Spence, "I can't say I have."

"Well, I have, and I can assure you it's no fun at all. Of course I dare say it's all mechanised now — no more picks and shovels and all that — but even so, it's jolly hard work, and personally I don't begrudge the miners a penny. Neither did Churchill, of course — I always remember that. But I don't suppose you've come here to talk about strikes!"

Spence smiled. "No," he said, "I'm afraid not."

Susan Green started to rise to her feet. "Would you like me to go?" she asked Spence.

"No, no, please stay. I'd like you to hear what I have to say."

"Oh. Right. Thank you." Susan sat down again. She seemed more composed than when Spence had last spoken to her, and sat in quite a relaxed position with her hands in her lap.

"Lady Dinnister," Spence began, "up to the present I've been working on the theory that the bottle of sherry which killed Miss Fosdyke was in fact intended for you."

"Oh. And isn't that the case?"

"No," said Spence. "For better or for worse, I am now quite certain that you were not the intended victim. Miss Fosdyke was."

"Oh dear," said Lady Dinnister. "Oh dear. I'm not quite sure how I feel about that. But what about that label you found — the compliments slip?"

"It was a fake. It certainly wasn't sent by Williams and Williams, and I now believe it was put there to mislead us."

"Oh dear," said Lady Dinnister again. She sighed heavily. "I don't know what to think about all this. It's a terrible business, it really is. In a way I felt better about it when I thought someone was trying to kill me … At my age any distraction is welcome, and the thought of being a potential murder victim was exciting in a perverse sort of way. But then I did feel terribly guilty about poor Emily drinking something that was intended for me. And now it seems I don't need to feel guilty at all because it was intended for her all along."

Spence nodded. "Yes, I'm afraid so."

"But why would anyone want to kill poor Emily?"

"That's what I want to ask you."

Lady Dinnister cupped her hands around her cheeks for a moment and then rubbed her eyes wearily. "Well, I don't know. What are the usual motives?"

"Well — apart from a sudden burst of uncontrollable anger — greed is a common motive. Also revenge, for some real or imagined offence. Jealousy, of course. And sexual motives."

"Yes. I see," said Lady Dinnister. "How about greed then? Well, as far as I know, Emily hadn't got much money to leave to anyone, and what she did have goes to her sister in Newcastle. She owned a bungalow and had some small savings, and that's about all. Revenge — well, who can she possibly have offended?"

"She spoke her mind quite freely." suggested Spence. "How about that?"

"Yes, well, we all speak our minds. But she could never have done anything cruel or malicious. She wasn't like that at all."

"So if she did cause someone grave offence, it must have been unwittingly?"

"Yes. Either that, or they were up to no good. I mean I have no doubt she would have reported a crime or something, that sort of thing. And I suppose that might cause someone to want to get their own back."

"Did she ever discuss any such incident with you?"

"No. I can't say she did. We would chat about all sorts of things, of course — all kinds of experiences that we'd had. But she never mentioned anything criminal."

"What about jealousy?" asked Spence.

Lady Dinnister frowned. "I can't imagine that it's relevant. Or a sexual motive, either. I mean, she was a single woman, sixty years of age. She wasn't the type to go around stealing someone's husband."

"Nevertheless," said Spence, "the fact is that someone hated or feared her badly enough to set out to poison her deliberately. And the indications are that it was someone here in this house — or at any rate with easy access to it."

Lady Dinnister's face grew pale, and she said nothing for a moment. But. surprisingly enough, Susan Green spoke up.

"The fact is. Superintendent, nobody here liked Miss Fosdyke very much. Apart from Lady Dinnister, that is."

Spence turned to look at Susan. In marked contrast to her earlier manner, she now seemed quite confident.

"I mean," Susan continued, "if we're going to help you at all, we've got to be really honest and truthful, haven't we?"

"Certainly."

"Well, if I were to be completely honest about it, I'd have to say that I didn't like Miss Fosdyke very much myself."

"Why not?"

"Well, as I've already told you, she disapproved of my relationship with Alec. And I didn't think that was really any of her business. And, although I didn't fall out with her about it, I was pretty upset. In fact, not to put too fine a point on it, I disliked her very much indeed."

"Badly enough to kill her?"

Susan's eyes widened, but she remained calm. "Well no, no, of course not. But the point I'm trying to make to you is that the staff here generally felt pretty much the same. We got on all right with her because you have to work with people — but we didn't really like her. Any of us."

"Any particular reason?"

"No, I can't say there was anything specific. It was just her manner."

Lady Dinnister rejoined the conversation. "Emily could be a bit standoffish," she admitted. "A bit arrogant, I suppose. And now that I think about it, I realise that Dr. Milton didn't care for her much either."

"Do you know why?"

"No, not really. I think it was just that, having worked in a hospital for forty years, Emily thought she knew quite a lot about medicine. And doctors don't like that attitude, you know. They like to feel that they're the experts. They seem to think that everyone else should do what they tell them without asking questions."

"Could I ask what your family thought about Miss Fosdyke? Edward, and Alec, and your granddaughter, for instance?"

Lady Dinnister smiled ruefully. "I don't think they liked her at all!" she said. "Not now you mention it. Of course, they didn't have to see much of her. She was my companion, and I liked her very much indeed. But Elizabeth, for one, couldn't stand her — oil and water, you know, from the very beginning. And Edward and Alec, of course, they had nothing whatever in common with her."

"And she opposed the idea of your selling Marlby Manor?"

"Yes. Yes, she did, come to think of it. And if they thought she influenced me on that, then I suppose that was yet another reason for them disliking her. But not — surely not — not to the point where they would want to murder her, Mr. Spence. I mean, I know my family better than anyone, and I would stake my life on it. None of them would even think of such a thing."

Spence made no comment, but inwardly he wished that he could have a pound for every time he had heard similar statements made.

"Let me ask you about Monday evening," Spence continued. "In particular, I want to know where people were. As far as you know, were Mr. Tanner, Mr. Jones, and Miss Quinn all in the manor that evening?"

Lady Dinnister paused, looking upwards to think. "Well, yes, as far as I know. I know of no reason why they shouldn't have been here."

"And were they all here on Tuesday?"

"Oh yes, they were certainly here then. Weren't they, Susan?"

"Definitely," Susan agreed.

"Now what about your family — Edward and Alec and Elizabeth and Vernon. Did any of them visit the manor on Monday night?"

Lady Dinnister shook her head. "No. Definitely not. Well, I say definitely. If they did come here, they didn't come and see me."

"And they would do so normally?"

"Well, yes. I mean, Alec comes occasionally to see Susan rather than me, but even then he normally drops in to say hello."

"All right. And what about on Tuesday?"

"Oh, they were all here then. That was the day we found poor Emily, so they all came at one time or another to see how I was."

Spence directed his next question at Susan Green. "You usually keep your filing cabinets locked, don't you?"

"Usually, yes."

"Did Miss Fosdyke ever ask you for the keys, or ask to look at any of the files you keep on the staff?"

"No, never. Why do you ask?"

"Oh, just a thought," said Spence. "Just a thought." He turned back to Lady Dinnister. "I remember you telling me that Miss Fosdyke used to let her bungalow from time to time."

"Yes, that's right."

"And at the moment it's empty?"

"Yes."

"Do you know where the keys to the bungalow are now?"

"Yes, they're among her possessions. We sorted them out on Tuesday."

"Do you think I could borrow them?" asked Spence. "I'd like to look round the bungalow — see if I can find anything useful among her papers."

"Yes, by all means. Susan, you know where the keys are, don't you? Would you be kind enough to get them, please?"

"Yes, of course," said Susan. She got up and left the room.

After Susan had gone, Lady Dinnister sighed very deeply. "All this talk of hatred and fear," she said with distaste. "Somehow I can't equate all that with Emily. I accept that the staff here didn't like her very much. I accept that my family didn't find her all that enthralling. And I could find fault with her myself if I wanted to; she was a bit of a snob, and she had strong views, and she didn't sulfer fools gladly. But we're none of us perfect, and I found her a most helpful and acceptable companion. The fact is I *need* someone like Fosdyke. I needed her very badly. She was intelligent and cultured and a good conversationalist, and she was a damn good nurse, even though she wasn't qualified as one. And she wasn't afraid of hard work. And for all her faults, she was a good Christian woman — we went to communion together regularly. I can't believe that anyone would hate her and try to kill her. Why on earth would they do such a thing?"

Spence stood up to go. "It's all a question of perspective," he said. "It depends on where you're standing. You see, if Miss Fosdyke performed an act of kindness for you, she may, knowingly or unknowingly, have caused the most deadly offence to someone else, either by commission or omission. What I have to do is to identify what that act was, and who the someone else is."

"And you think it's someone close to me — someone here in my household?" asked Lady Dinnister with sadly troubled eyes.

"Yes," said Spence. "I'm afraid I do."

Twenty-Three

Spence went downstairs again in search of Laurel. He found him in the kitchen, talking to Hazel.

While Spence had been with Lady Dinnister, Laurel had spoken to Len Jones, Alfred Tanner, and finally to Hazel, and had established that all three had been in the manor on Monday evening. None of them had gone out, and none of them had heard or seen any visitors.

"So, where to now?" asked Laurel after he had reported his findings to Spence.

Spence scratched his chin and thought about it. "Well, I think we'll go to Lime Beach," he said after a moment. "Miss Fosdyke had a bungalow there, and I'd like to look round it."

After collecting the keys to Miss Fosdyke's bungalow from Susan Green, Spence and Laurel left Marlby and drove twelve miles to Lime Beach, on the coast. There, at the end of a rather twee cul-de-sac, they located the home to which Miss Fosdyke had hoped, one day, to retire.

As they got out of the car, net curtains in at least two other houses in the cul-de-sac fluttered almost imperceptibly as sharp-eyed neighbours examined the visitors.

"Amazing," said Spence. "Even the bourgeoisie can spot a copper these days."

"Oh, I don't know," said Laurel with a grin. "Perhaps they think we're villains."

Spence smiled back. "Well, if they do, no doubt we shall have a Panda car round before very long. Let's wait and see."

The two men let themselves into the bungalow via the front door, and after a preliminary walk through the whole house they decided to begin their search in the living room.

"Are we looking for anything specific?" asked Laurel. "Or just what leaps out at us?"

"The latter mostly," said Spence. "This whole visit is a bit of a long shot. I don't really expect to find anything useful, but you never know what dreadful secrets you might turn up. Miss Fosdyke might have been secretly married, for instance. And if she was married, presumably the man concerned would inherit this bungalow and anything else she may have owned. Which might, for some people, be a powerful motive."

For some time the two men searched in silence, moving from the living room to the other rooms of the house, and finally to the loft and the garage. At the end of an hour and a half, they had very little to show for their efforts.

Spence returned to the living room and looked through the few items that he had put on one side as worthy of a second glance. A few minutes later Laurel joined him.

"Well," said Spence with a sigh, "there isn't much here. The main item is a will, which was signed a few months ago."

"And who gets Miss Fosdyke's money?"

"Her sister. Gets the lot, in fact. House, money, and all sundries."

"Oh," said Laurel interestedly. "So the sister has a motive then?"

"Well, a motive of sorts, yes. She lives up in Newcastle, so you'd better get the police up there to check on her whereabouts on Monday and Tuesday. Just for the record. But I'll give you a hundred to one it's a dead end."

"Anything else?"

"A couple of building society account books, showing that she had a nice little nest egg tucked away. And that's about it."

"What about all those letters?" asked Laurel, pointing to a pile of correspondence that Spence had unearthed. "Anything in those?"

"Nothing much. They're like the ones we found in her room at the manor: mostly idle gossip about nephews and nieces. There is just one with a flicker of promise." Spence picked up a piece of blue notepaper and passed it to Laurel. "It seems to be from a pharmacist, or possibly a doctor, who's working at Wellbridge General. It was originally sent to Marlby Manor. As far as I can see, Miss Fosdyke must have written to this man asking for his comments on a certain type of treatment for high blood pressure. As you can see, he wrote back very cagily, saying it all depended on the patient, and so on and so forth, but by and large he wouldn't think that the treatment described was very suitable for an elderly lady."

"Yes," Laurel agreed, "that does look promising. Suppose, for the sake of argument, that Lady Dinnister was the one being treated for high blood pressure, and suppose Miss Fosdyke didn't think she was being given the right drugs — then, knowing what we do of old Fosdyke, it seems likely that she would have had it out with the doctor concerned. Dr. Milton, wasn't it?"

Spence nodded. "Yes. And since Lady Dinnister is no doubt a private patient, Dr. Milton might have been very annoyed indeed at anyone poking their nose into his professional relationship with her."

"And if, as a result of all that, Lady Dinnister lost confidence in him and went elsewhere for treatment, Dr. Milton might find himself with a significant loss of income."

"Yes, that's right."

"So perhaps we ought to call on Dr. Milton and see what he says?" suggested Laurel.

"Not a bad idea," Spence agreed, rising to his feet. "It's not much of a lead, but it's all we've got to show for the best part of a morning's work."

Twenty-Four

A telephone call to Dr. Milton established that it would be convenient for him to see them at the end of morning surgery, in about twenty minutes' time. The two detectives drove to Lower Durwood and called at the local post office for directions.

Dr. Milton's consulting rooms proved to be in part of his own house, which was a former rectory. The rectory was a large, rambling, and apparently not very well-maintained building; outside, the lawns needed cutting, and the hedge had not been trimmed for some years; inside, however, the waiting room was light, spacious, and airy.

After ten minutes Dr. Milton's last patient of the morning departed, and he emerged from his surgery and invited Spence and Laurel to come in.

Dr. Milton's desk and chair were in a corner on the far side of the room. One chair for patients was positioned in front of the desk, to the right, and turned sideways on. The only other chair in the room was against the wall on the left and clearly only intended for use on very rare occasions.

Spence did not care for this arrangement at all. It was his experience that solicitors, doctors, and other professional men frequently positioned the furniture in their offices so as to make their clients and visitors feel ill at ease, and hence more likely to accept the advice that was provided without question or debate. Whether Dr. Milton had deliberately set out his chairs with this aim in mind, Spence didn't know, but he took no chances. He seized the chair in front of the desk and moved it several feet, so that when sitting in it he would have his back to the window; this would place him in a far more dominant position than Dr. Milton himself, despite the presence of that formidable desk. Laurel took his lead from Spence and moved the other chair so that he was sitting beside Spence and thus appeared to be reinforcing the attack.

It was obvious that Dr. Milton did not like this furniture-moving operation one bit. His eyebrows rose, and he fiddled nervously with a pencil; for a second his mouth opened as if he were about to speak, but he evidently thought better of it.

"Well, Dr. Milton," Spence began briskly, "I won't waste any more of your time than I have to. As I explained to you on the phone, my colleague and I are investigating the murder of Miss Emily Fosdyke, and what we'd like to know, basically, is why you didn't like her."

Dr. Milton looked astonished, as well he might. As a country doctor, he was used to having his word taken as gospel ninety-nine percent of the time; it was very seldom that anyone questioned his judgement, and then only very tentatively. The experience of having two large and apparently very rude detectives bursting into his office, moving his chairs about, and making very pointed remarks was entirely new to him. For the moment it threw him completely off balance — which was, of course, exactly what Spence had intended.

"I — er — I don't quite understand," said Dr. Milton hesitantly. "I didn't dislike Miss Fosdyke at all. Not at all."

"Oh, come now," said Spence sharply. "We've already taken statements from a number of people, and they all comment on the fact that relations between you and Miss Fosdyke were distinctly cool."

"Well, I'm sorry," said Dr. Milton apologetically, "but I can't imagine who these people are or what they're referring to."

Spence sighed. "Dr. Milton," he said patiently, "it's getting near lunchtime, and my stomach is beginning to rumble. I had hoped that this interview would be all over in ten minutes but, if you insist, we can take an hour over it, or maybe two. I have always taken the view that it was in my own best interests to be frank with my doctor whenever I consulted him, and I can assure you that exactly the same principle applies when people talk to the police. Now, I repeat: why did you not like Miss Fosdyke?"

Dr. Milton looked down at his desk for a moment. His already ruddy complexion had turned an even darker red, although whether from anger or embarrassment it was not yet clear. Eventually he looked up and stared Spence straight in the eye; it was now obvious that he was very angry indeed and had fully recovered his nerve.

"Very well," he said loudly. "Since you insist, I will answer your extremely impertinent and offensive question. I'll tell you why I disliked Miss Fosdyke. But I will do so solely on the understanding that I could also enumerate several reasons as to why I admired her and why I valued her skill and experience as a medical social worker. Is that agreed?"

"It is."

"Very well." Dr. Milton lowered his voice a decibel or two and cleared his throat. "Well now, I disliked Miss Fosdyke primarily because she was officious. And I'm talking about her professional life now. She spent forty years working at Wellbridge General Hospital, and she inevitably accumulated a great deal of power and authority. She knew all the consultants well, and of course she'd been there far longer than most of them. This gave her an inflated view of her own role and importance. In my experience she was often arrogant, rude, and condescending."

"You crossed swords with her then?"

"On several occasions, yes. Whenever I sent her a patient with a problem, she seemed to regard it as a personal affront, despite the fact that she was being paid to sort those problems out. As a result, I did not always rush to sort problems out when she brought them to me. Consequently, we did not get on."

"Let's be more specific," said Spence, "and more up-to-date. What did you think of Miss Fosdyke's influence on Lady Dinnister?"

Dr. Milton paused and tapped his pencil on the desk in front of him. "It was both good and bad," he said after a moment.

"Elaborate, please."

"Well, it was good in the sense that she stamped on any incipient hypochondria, and she encouraged the right mental attitude. She saw to it that Lady Dinnister had regular hours, regular meals, and suitable exercise. On the bad side — well, she tended to think that she knew more about medicine than any doctor."

"She disputed your diagnosis, did she?"

"No. Fortunately," Dr. Milton continued dryly, "we were both agreed that Lady Dinnister had high blood pressure and arthritis."

"But she disagreed with you over the appropriate treatment?"

"She did, yes. She tended to think that a fancy diet would be more effective than drugs."

"Did she argue with you about it?"

"Not so much argue as harangue. In her usual arrogant way, she asked me if I was familiar with all the latest research on these conditions. She quoted the names of various so-called experts at me."

"And what did you say?"

"I told her that I preferred to base my treatment on something more authoritative than an article in the *Reader's Digest.*"

Spence smiled. "That wasn't very tactful, was it?"

"No, and it wasn't very tactful of Miss Fosdyke to question my treatment."

"Would it surprise you to know that she had written to former medical colleagues at the hospital, asking for their comments on what you were prescribing?"

"No, it wouldn't surprise me at all. But it would surprise me very much indeed if any of them had given her any encouragement to argue with me. Deciding the right treatment for a patient depends very much on knowing that patient, and I greatly resent any half-baked amateurs trying to interfere in my professional affairs."

"And how long have you been Lady Dinnister's doctor?"

"Ten years."

"She's a private patient?"

"Yes."

"Where were you on Monday evening?"

Dr. Milton turned his head sideways to think. "Monday evening," he muttered. "This week?"

"Yes."

"Well ... after surgery I played squash with the vicar." Spence nodded and returned to his original line of questioning. "Did Miss Fosdyke ever suggest to Lady Dinnister that she should seek a second medical opinion?"

"If she did, I never heard about it."

"And how would you have felt about it if you had?"

Dr. Milton took a deep breath and drew himself up. He placed his hands flat on the desk in front of him. "Well, quite frankly, and I don't know whether you will believe this or not, but I couldn't possibly have cared less."

"Why not? Surely if Lady Dinnister had left you and gone to some other doctor, you would have lost a considerable income in fees?"

"Not as much as you might think. And, in any case, it can be rather tedious being at the constant beck and call of an imperious old lady."

"Has Lady Dinnister left you any money in her will?"

The doctor gave a short laugh of astonishment. "Well, if she has, she's certainly never mentioned it."

"How hard up are you, Doctor?"

Dr. Milton frowned and leaned forward again. Any trace of nervousness or hesitancy had long since disappeared; he was now feeling openly aggressive. "That's a pretty insulting remark, even by your standards. Why don't you just come straight out and ask me if I was the one who tried to poison Lady Dinnister?"

"Well, were you?"

"No, I was not!" Dr. Milton was almost shouting again.

"And what's the answer to my question?"

"What question?"

"How hard up are you?"

Dr. Milton gritted his teeth before answering. "Look — I've got two sons at very expensive schools, I run two cars, I've got a twenty-five-thousand-pound mortgage, and I'm sitting here wearing a shirt with frayed cuffs. How hard up do you think I am?"

Twenty-Five

"Well!" said Spence cheerfully, rubbing his hands together. "That was a bit more like it, wasn't it? I like a man with a bit of spirit; makes the day a lot more interesting."

The two detectives were walking back to Spence's car after their interview with Dr. Milton. Spence unlocked the door of his Granada and climbed in. Laurel slipped into the front seat beside him.

"What do you think about him claiming to be hard up?" said Laurel. "I thought that was a bit steep. I wouldn't consider myself hard up on his salary."

"Well, no, but it's all according to circumstances, isn't it?" said Spence. "Expenditure has a nasty way of rising up to and beyond whatever your income is. No, I think he was being honest enough at that point; he probably is a bit hard-pressed financially. The problem is: is that a strong enough motive?"

"But he wouldn't gain directly from Miss Fosdyke's death," Laurel pointed out. "And we know now that she was definitely the intended victim."

"Yes, agreed," said Spence. "But Dr. Milton might gain indirectly, as you yourself pointed out earlier on. Suppose, for instance, that Lady Dinnister was paying him a retaining fee, if they have such things in medical circles. And suppose for the moment that Miss Fosdyke was persuading her to change doctors. Well, in that case he would lose a valuable patient, and he might quite easily lose others because Lady Dinnister no doubt has friends and relations who would be influenced by her views."

"It was a clumsy method of killing someone, though," said Laurel. "For a doctor, I mean. Surely a doctor could find a more effective method of murdering someone than giving them arsenic?"

"Well, perhaps he wouldn't want to," said Spence. "If the method were too sophisticated, then of course we would immediately know who'd done it, wouldn't we? Anyway, let's go and have some lunch and think about it."

Spence drove half a mile to the Durwood Arms, a pub on the road to Wellbridge. Before leaving Miss Fosdyke's bungalow, he had telephoned his wife and asked her to meet him there for lunch. On arrival he now telephoned Detective Sergeant Wilberforce to report his latest location, in case he should need to be reached urgently.

Julia had already arrived at the pub, having driven from Wellbridge in her blue Mini. She was waiting for them in the saloon bar, where they joined her for a quick drink. Then they retired to a small private room called the snuggery, where Spence had booked lunch for them in circumstances which would ensure that their conversation was not overheard.

Over a first course of fruit juices, Spence told his wife how he and Laurel had spent the morning, thus bringing her up to date on developments in the case so far. While the main course was being disposed of, discussion was kept to a minimum but, having decided to skip dessert, they got down to business again over coffee.

"Right," said Spence. "So here we are then. We've established that Miss Fosdyke was quite definitely the person who was intended to be murdered all along, and not Lady Dinnister, so what we're doing now is looking for motives for the murder of Miss Fosdyke. The means of committing the crime remain exactly the same as before: arsenic. And at least ten people, if we include the doctor, could have had easy access to the arsenic in the gardener's shed and could have walked in and out of the house on Monday evening without too many questions being asked. So, as I say, what it really boils down to is a question of motive. Let's go through the suspects one by one. First, Lady Dinnister."

"Lady Dinnister?" said Julia in surprise.

"Yes, and why not, pray?"

"Well, if she wanted to get rid of Miss Fosdyke, I should have thought it would have been a whole lot easier to sack her."

"Perhaps she couldn't sack her."

"Why not?"

"Well," said Spence, "one can hypothesize all sorts of reasons. Incriminating evidence of some kind. Perhaps Miss Fosdyke was blackmailing her. Or perhaps sacking was felt to be an insufficient punishment — perhaps she was morbidly jealous of Miss Fosdyke."

"But from what you've said," Julia persisted, "Lady Dinnister sounds much too well balanced for that."

"Well, maybe she is," said Spence grudgingly. "But I just don't think we should rule her out entirely, that's all."

"Oh, all right then," said Julia. "But let's talk about the doctor. He sounds much more promising. As far as I can see, he's the only one who had really serious rows with Miss Fosdyke."

"Yes," said Spence, "that's true. The trouble is, he seems to have a pretty good alibi for Monday evening." He turned to Laurel. "We really must find out how much Lady Dinnister was paying him. Remind me to ask Susan Green; I expect she'll know. And once we've got that piece of information, we'll know how seriously to take him as a suspect."

Laurel nodded. "What about Susan Green herself?" he asked. "She had a disagreement with Miss Fosdyke too, although she alleges it was quite amicable."

"Yes, and it involves real passion," said Spence. "After all, Susan is apparently head-over-heels in love with young Alec, and here's this nosy old ratbag telling her she doesn't approve. It's enough to make anyone poison your sherry, wouldn't you say so, Julia?"

"Well, since you ask," said Julia, "no. I think you're confusing the fury of a woman scorned with the attitude of a woman — namely Susan Green — who really didn't need to take any notice whatever of Miss Fosdyke. If Miss Fosdyke hadn't died, Susan's love affair with Alec would still have proceeded quite naturally, with both parties making up their own minds either to get married or to call the whole thing off, regardless of what Miss Fosdyke thought. She had no real influence on the matter one way or the other."

"Well, perhaps so," said Spence. "But she apparently did have some influence on this business of the sale of the manor. Now there's a half-million-pound motive if ever I saw one."

"Yes, that is a bit more promising," said Julia. "With Fosdyke gone, Edward could presumably persuade his mother-in-law to sell the manor after all."

"But Edward doesn't benefit directly," Laurel reminded them.

"No," said Spence, "but his children do. And for all we know, he may have done a private deal with them. 'I persuade Granny, you give me half of the money' — that sort of thing."

"Alec Bannerman, in fact, has two motives," suggested Laurel. "First of all, Miss Fosdyke was blocking the sale of the manor, so he would be against her for that reason and, secondly, she was interfering in his relationship with Susan Green."

"Ah, but he didn't know that," said Spence.

"Well, that's what he and Miss Green *say*, yes," Laurel agreed. "But don't you think it's much more likely that Susan went and wept on his shoulder, and told him what that nasty old Fosdyke had been saying to her?"

"Fair point," Spence admitted. "Fair point. The other grandchild, Elizabeth Hassett, has an even clearer motive still. She and her husband are obviously badly in need of some ready cash — or so I would judge — and Fosdyke is one of the main obstacles to their getting what they want … Now, that just leaves us with the household staff: Hazel, Len Jones — he of the prominent jaw — and Mr. Tanner, the butler. And while they all had rather good motives for attempting to murder Lady Dinnister, none of them, so far as we know, had any reason at all to dispose of Miss Fosdyke."

"Apart from the fact that none of them liked her very much," said Laurel.

"Yes, apart from that." Spence looked at his two companions. "Well, it's make-your-mind-up time, folks. Pick a winner, please." He looked expectantly at Laurel.

"You want me to say who did it?" asked Laurel.

"I do."

"Oh. Well, if you insist, I pick Susan Green. And Alec Bannerman."

"Together?"

"Yes. Why not? That inheritance seems a powerful motive to me. And love is akin to madness, after all; they could have infected each other."

"All right. Julia?"

Julia frowned. "The problem is, I haven't met them in person," she said doubtfully. "I've only heard about these people secondhand."

"Don't evade the issue," said Spence sternly.

"You remember what I said about the consequences of not killing Miss Fosdyke having to seem far worse than the consequences of actually doing it?" asked Julia. "That sense of desperation has to be there, but I don't get that feeling about any of the suspects. Not yet."

"But, if you had to commit yourself," said Spence, "with reservations … "

There was a pause. Then, "It must be a man," Julia said suddenly. "And that's all I'm saying for the moment … What about you, Ben? Who do you fancy?"

Spence opened his mouth to answer but was interrupted by a knock on the door. "Come in," he called.

The waiter put his head into the room. "Excuse me, Mr. Spence, but there's a telephone call for you. A Mr. Wilberforce."

"Oh, right," said Spence. He glanced at the others. "Excuse me."

Spence left the snuggery and went out into the hall, where the telephone receiver was lying on a small table.

"Hello?" he said.

"Oh, sorry to interrupt your lunch, sir," said Detective Sergeant Wilberforce, "but I've just had a call from Mr. Bannerman — Mr. Edward Bannerman."

"Oh? What did he say?"

"He said he'd be very grateful if you'd go round and see him as soon as possible, sir."

"I see. Did he say why?"

"Yes, sir. He said he wanted to confess."

Twenty-Six

Not surprisingly, in view of this intriguing telephone message, Spence and Laurel rapidly finished their coffee and drove immediately to the village of Hattley, in order to call on Edward Bannerman. Julia Spence drove herself home.

When they arrived at the Bannermans' house in Hattley, Spence rang the bell. It echoed distantly within the house, and there was a long, long pause before anything happened. Then, just as Spence was about to ring again, the door was opened.

It was opened by Hazel Quinn.

"Oh," said Spence in surprise. "Good afternoon."

"Afternoon, Superintendent," said Hazel placidly. She blinked at him through her glasses with her oddly crossed eyes.

Spence blinked back for a moment, and with every justification. Hazel was wearing a white silk robe that was tied around her waist with a sash of the same material. It was almost transparent, and it clung to her body, revealing quite clearly that she was wearing nothing else underneath.

"We — er — we've come to see Mr. Bannerman," said Spence slowly. He was temporarily somewhat distracted from his main line of thought.

"Yes, that's right," Hazel agreed. "He is expecting you. He's in the studio at the moment. Come along in."

She stood to one side to allow the two detectives to enter, and then, having closed the door behind them, led the way to the back of the house.

The view of Hazel from the rear was, if anything, even more spectacular than the view from the front, and Spence winked broadly at Laurel, who grinned happily in return as they followed on.

"The policemen are here," said Hazel as they reached their destination.

"Oh, good, good, bring them in," said Edward. He was standing over on the right of the studio, hard at work on a canvas placed on an easel in front of him. "I won't keep you more than a few moments," he continued. "But I must just finish what I'm doing while the paint's wet."

"That's all right," said Spence. "No rush."

A few feet in front of the easel, a red velvet curtain had been draped from a hook on the wall, with its folds carefully arranged. On the floor were one or two Greek-looking vases, with potted plants on either side. The only thing missing was the artist's model, who had clearly been standing in front of this backdrop.

"Would you like me to pose again?" asked Hazel.

"No, no, that's all right," said Edward. "I've nearly finished. And in any case, it might embarrass our visitors."

"Oh, don't let us interfere with your work," said Spence hastily.

Edward laughed. "No. No, I wouldn't do that, I can assure you. But I do genuinely want a break. We haven't had lunch yet, and I'm tired. Hazel, be an angel and see if you can find us something to eat while I'm talking to these gentlemen."

"Okay." Hazel smiled and disappeared at a leisurely pace toward the kitchen.

Spence walked across the studio and stood behind Edward Bannerman as he finished off what he was doing. The picture in progress was a full-length nude study of a woman who was quite clearly recognisable as Hazel Quinn without her glasses. The eyes were demurely cast down, so the artist had not had to idealise their fearsome difference of direction. The whole work, though unfinished, had considerable erotic power.

"Well?" said Edward. "What do you think?"

Spence was genuinely impressed. "It's a remarkable piece of work," he said warmly. "If you ever need a home for it, I'm sure we could find one somewhere at headquarters."

"Perhaps in the canteen?" suggested Laurel, who had also sneaked a look.

Edward chuckled, still dabbing away at one corner of the painting with a brush. "No, I'm afraid you can't have it, either of you, because it's spoken for. It was commissioned by a club in London, as a matter of fact. What they wanted was something erotic yet not pornographic — old-fashioned if you like, the kind of thing the Victorians used to go in for."

"I'm sure they'll be delighted with it," said Spence.

Edward put down his brush with a sigh. "Yes, well, I do have a very good model. And that's half the battle." He seized a rag and wiped his hands on it briefly. "Still, I haven't asked you here to talk about my work, fascinating though it may be."

Edward crossed to the other side of the studio, where there was an old couch with the stuffing beginning to leak out of it, together with two other rickety chairs. He motioned for his visitors to sit down.

"Make yourselves comfortable," he said. "But watch out for the springs."

"Thanks ... Well now," said Spence, when they were all seated, "you sent a message asking us to call on you."

"Yes."

"Something about ... wanting to confess?"

"Yes," said Edward doubtfully. "Yes, that's right. That's what I did say. Tell me ... " he paused. "Miss Fosdyke was poisoned with arsenic, wasn't she?"

"That's common knowledge," said Spence. "It's been reported in all the newspapers."

"Yes." Edward paused again. "I've been reading quite a lot about poisons recently. And dying of arsenic can't have been very pleasant."

"No," Spence agreed. "But strychnine would have been worse, of course."

"Yes, I can imagine. I've read about it. There are better methods. Did you know, for instance, that an intracardiac injection of Thiopentone causes permanent cessation of breathing within two seconds?"

"No," said Spence. "I can't say I did."

"Well, it does. And how do I come to know that? Well, I don't want to go all dramatic on you, Superintendent, but the fact is, I'm going to die. Of course, you're going to die too, but in my case I can set a fairly precise date to it. A year from now at the very most. Quite possibly less. Occasionally, over the past few months, I've thought I was getting better. But I'm told — and I have to believe it — that that's an illusion. A temporary remission which won't last very long. And I certainly don't feel all that clever. I feel tired, and ill, and depressed."

"So," said Spence quietly, "that's why you've been studying poisons."

"Yes. I'm very fond of life, Superintendent — very fond of it indeed. But I don't fancy a slow, lingering death. When the time comes, I think I'd prefer to go like switching out a light before you go to bed."

"That's understandable," said Spence. "And did you apply this newfound knowledge of yours to murdering Miss Fosdyke?"

There was a long pause before Edward answered.

"No," he said eventually. "No, I didn't ... I must apologise, Superintendent, for that rather gimmicky phone call. I did want to speak to you, and I thought a message like that would get you here fairly quickly. And for a while ... Well, I must ask you to forgive me. Perhaps it's my illness, or perhaps it's just that I'm fundamentally not very bright, but for a while I did toy with the idea of confessing that I had murdered Miss Fosdyke."

"Because," said Spence, "you're afraid that one of your children might be responsible."

Edward looked down at the floor and smiled. "Yes," he said. "You don't miss much, do you? It's not an easy thing for me to admit, believe me. It's one of the hardest things I've ever had to face in my life. But I know a little bit about human nature, and half a million pounds is a very big temptation. That's what they'd get, you see, if my mother-in-law sold the manor. Half a million pounds, at least. And there's no doubt in my mind that Fosdyke was the chief obstacle to that sale. She had a very great influence on Lady Dinnister, even though the old girl didn't like to admit it. Without Fosdyke there, I'm sure I could talk Lady Dinnister round. As things stand, you see, she may live for another twenty or even thirty years. And that's a long time to wait for your money, Superintendent. Particularly when you're young. When I look back and think what I could have done if I'd had financial freedom at my children's age — well, I begin to understand what temptation is."

"Do either your son or your daughter have artistic ambitions?"

"No, no, they're not artistic at all, not in that sense. But they both have hopes and plans, you know. Things they would like to do if they had the money. Elizabeth wants to run a boutique, for example. Whether she'll be any good at it is a different matter, but that's what she wants to do. Alec — well, like a lot of young men, he's rather keen on cars. Maybe he'll be an engineer — or maybe he'll end up running a string of garages."

"Well," said Spence, "I'm glad for both our sakes that you didn't try to make a false confession. It would have been a futile waste of everyone's time, and we should have tripped you up pretty quickly."

"What, you mean by asking me how much poison I used, how it was administered, that kind of thing?"

"Yes."

"Yes, I suppose you would. Anyway, the idea passed out of my head almost as soon as it came in. I suppose what I really wanted to do — why I really wanted to get you here — was to find out whether my fears are groundless or not."

"Well, I may be able to help you there," said Spence. "To start with, you can tell me where your son was on Monday evening between about six o'clock and eleven."

"Monday evening," said Edward slowly. "Let me see now … Monday evening. Yes, I remember — Alec was here with me all evening."

"You're sure now? He couldn't have gone out at all? Not while you were dozing or anything?"

"No, he didn't go out. I wasn't feeling too well that night, so he sat with me most of the time, reading. He made me a meal at about eight o'clock, I remember. But why is Monday evening so important?"

"I think I'll keep the details of that to myself," said Spence. "But what I can tell you is that if Alec was here with you, as you say, then he can't possibly have killed Miss Fosdyke."

"Oh, I see," said Edward. His expression was grave. "Well, that's some comfort, anyway."

"Is there anyone else who can vouch for his presence here?"

"No. No, I'm afraid there isn't. Do we need anyone else?"

"Not at the moment, no. But it's always useful to have two independent witnesses. What about your daughter?"

"Elizabeth?" Edward paused again. "Well, Elizabeth is a married woman, Superintendent. She lives with her husband."

"Have you any idea where they were on Monday night?"

Edward shook his head slowly. "No. No, I'm afraid I haven't. That's something that you'll have to take up with them."

"Don't worry," said Spence. "I will."

Twenty-Seven

Toward three o'clock Spence and Laurel returned to the police house at Marlby, where they made a cup of tea and sat down to think.

"Anything new come in?" Spence asked Detective Sergeant Wilberforce, who had been manning the office all morning.

"One or two things," said Wilberforce, pulling a pile of reports toward him. "I sent a couple of men round to that farm where young Alec Bannerman has been working this summer, and they found an old tin of sheep dip, which is presumably arsenic."

"I believe it often is," said Spence. "How old was it?"

"Well, pretty ancient, I gather. They couldn't really tell if it had been opened recently, but we've sent a sample off to be analysed, so we'll know what it is before long."

Spence grunted. "Oh. Anything else?"

"Yes. We've run a couple of checks on Miss Fosdyke, along the lines you requested. Her sister in Newcastle can think of no possible family connection, however remote, between her and Len Jones, and there's no record at St. Catherine's House of Miss Fosdyke ever having been married."

"Oh," said Laurel. "So that business about the prominent jaw was just a coincidence, after all?"

"So it would seem," said Spence. "They don't seem to be members of the same family, anyway."

"Third thing," Wilberforce continued, "is that Mr. and Mrs. Hassett very definitely owe a lot of money, all over the place. Their bank manager, when questioned, threw up his hands in horror — which was eloquent enough, though he wasn't prepared to give any details, of course."

"Well, that's much as we expected," said Spence. "We could see they were spendthrifts at a glance. What have we learnt about where all our suspects were on Monday night, when the poison was put in the bottle?"

Wilberforce shuffled through his papers. "Well, Alec Bannerman says he was at home with his father."

"And his father says the same," Laurel commented.

"Which may or may not be reliable," said Spence. "After all, we know by his own admission that Edward was actively thinking of lying to us. So maybe he did, after all. What about the Hassetts?"

"At home, watching the TV," Wilberforce told him.

"Hmm, well, the same thing applies there. Either one of them could be covering up for the other, or they could have acted together."

Laurel nodded thoughtfully.

"Those are the only ones you asked me to check up on," said Wilberforce.

"Yes, that's right, but I can add a few more details to the file from this morning's discussions. Dr. Milton says he was playing squash with the vicar, but we'd better check that out. Find out what time surgery finished, whether he had a meal, the time he began playing squash — all that sort of thing. Susan Green claims she was at home all on her own, which is either true or a very clever piece of bluff. And the household staff were all on the premises. So, where does that get us?"

"As far as I can see," said Laurel, "it doesn't get us anywhere, really. All we've discovered is that the farm where Alec Bannerman worked is another possible source of the poison, and that none of our suspects has an absolutely reliable alibi."

"Yes, I'm afraid you're right," said Spence. "Which brings us back to motive, really, and the assessment of character ... Well, we've talked about motive at length, so let's try thinking about the depth of feeling involved. Which of the people we've been talking to is callous and selfish and desperate enough to kill at one remove? Not a face-to-face murder — which requires a very special kind of guts — or extreme provocation, but a murder by stealth and deception. Who do you think hated and feared Miss Fosdyke strongly enough to go to the trouble and risk of killing her?" He glanced at the faces of his two colleagues.

"I pass," said Wilberforce without hesitation.

Laurel frowned. "Well, the one thing that's abundantly clear is that there is no proof against anyone."

"Agreed," said Spence. "But are you sticking to your previous assessment — Alec Bannerman and Susan Green?"

"Yes," said Laurel slowly. "But I'm not convinced that I'm right."

"I am," said Spence firmly. "Convinced that I'm right, that is. I don't agree with your choice, I'm afraid — I find it hard to believe that those two young people were acting in concert — but I've made a choice of my own, based on my assessment of character, and I believe in my bones that the person I've got in mind is guilty. But of course I can't prove it. And what is worse, I have a nasty feeling that we're not going to be able to get any proof."

"Oh," said Laurel doubtfully. "So the murderer could get away with it?"

"I'm very much afraid so." Spence looked serious. "That's the trouble with poisoning cases; it's extremely difficult to be sure you've got the right person, and even more difficult to convince a jury."

There was silence for a few moments while Spence pondered over his problem.

"What do you propose to do then?" asked Laurel.

There was another pause before Spence answered. "Well," he said eventually, "if there's one thing that irks me beyond endurance, it's to see people getting away with murder, either literally or metaphorically. So if we haven't got any evidence, and if we aren't likely to get any by orthodox means, then we're just going to have to be a bit unorthodox."

"What, you mean provoke the murderer into betraying himself somehow?"

"Yes," said Spence. "You see, what we need is some kind of incontrovertible evidence. We need to goad the murderer into doing something which establishes his guilt beyond all reasonable doubt."

"How do you propose to do that?"

Spence hesitated again. "Well," he said with a grin, "I think the less you know about that, the better."

*

Spence drove off in his car and was gone for over two hours.

Detective Inspector Laurel, as befitted a loyal and conscientious officer, read through all the new reports, reread the old ones, tidied up the office, polished his shoes on a paper handkerchief, and was ultimately reduced to reading the adverts in the evening paper. Detective Sergeant Wilberforce pottered about happily, sticking coloured labels on his files and cross-indexing them.

At half past five that afternoon, Spence returned and declared that everything was now arranged.

"What do you mean, everything's arranged?" asked Laurel eagerly. "What's going on?"

Spence shook his head. "Well, I don't want to say too much. But to cut a long story short, I've persuaded Miss Green, who's a very cooperative young lady, to act as a kind of stalking-horse."

"Oh," said Laurel, with a trace of disappointment. "So that's the idea. Well, I hope you've got her well-protected, that's all."

"Oh yes, she's protected all right. Here's how it works ... " Spence sat down at his desk and leaned forward as he explained what was going to happen. "Susan Green has written a note, at my dictation, to the person who I believe murdered Miss Fosdyke."

"I see," said Laurel. "A sort of blackmail note, is it? 'I know you did it, so you'd better pay me or else' — that kind of thing?"

"No comment," said Spence with a grin. "All I will say is that the person to whom the letter is addressed has been invited to meet Miss Green at the summerhouse on the grounds of Marlby Manor, tonight at eleven o'clock."

"So — if he comes, we've got him cold," said Wilberforce.

"Not really," said Spence cautiously. "Even if he turns up, the person concerned could always say that he came just to clear his name."

"Or he could report the letter to us instead of going anywhere," said Laurel gloomily. "Adopt an attitude of outraged innocence."

"If he is bright enough, yes, he could," Spence admitted. "And then we really would be left high and dry. But with any luck, at about eleven o'clock tonight we shall be able to administer a very nasty shock to someone, and that's not a bad time to take a statement."

"Do you think you'll get a confession, sir?" asked Wilberforce.

"That's the idea, yes."

Laurel seemed very unconvinced by the whole operation, perhaps because he had not been allowed to know all the details. "Well," he said with a sigh, "it's a good idea if it works. All I can say is, I hope you've sent the letter to the right person."

"So do I," said Spence with feeling. "So do I."

Twenty-Eight

The evening passed slowly. For everyone.

Soon after his return to the police house, Spence sent Laurel home for a few hours. Later on he went out by himself for a quiet drink and a bite of supper at the Fishmonger's Arms.

When he came back at seven o'clock, Detective Sergeant Wilberforce placed in front of him an envelope that had been sent from Wellbridge General Hospital. It contained a folder extracted from the hospital files, a folder bearing the name of the only one of Spence's suspects who had had contact with Miss Fosdyke while she had been the hospital's almoner.

As soon as Spence withdrew the folder from the envelope and saw the name on it, he felt an enormous sense of relief. For, even before he read the folder's contents, he knew instinctively that his judgement had been sound.

It didn't take long to read Miss Fosdyke's notes. Her writing was small and rounded and neat, and her account of the patient's problems, and of his reaction to her attempts to deal with them, was concise, pithy, and, in places, amusing. In short, the contents of the folder confirmed all of Spence's suspicions. The original source of conflict between Miss Fosdyke and the patient was made quite clear. And it was easy to see how that conflict would have flared up again when Miss Fosdyke met the patient once more. The fear, the anger, and the bitterness which that meeting would have provoked were easy to imagine, and it was those very emotions, raised to new heights by the characters of the two individuals involved, that had motivated the murder.

After reading the folder, Spence closed it with a sigh and returned it to Wilberforce to be filed; if all went well that night, he would not need to refer to it again until after the murderer had been charged.

*

Darkness seemed to come slowly, at any rate for those members of the Southshire police force who were anxiously awaiting the hour of 11:00 P.M. The sun had shone all day, almost without break, and it descended very reluctantly into the west, casting a bright orange glow over the few clouds on the distant horizon.

In Marlby Manor, Lady Dinnister alternately watched television and tried to read; she was restless and ill at ease, without really knowing why. Elsewhere in the house, Len Jones, Hazel Quinn, and Alfred Tanner all busied themselves with minor tasks or else relaxed as best they could after a long, hot day.

In Hattley, five miles away, Edward and Alec Bannerman tinkered with the engine of an old Morris Minor until the failing light made them decide to call it a day and go indoors. In Foxford, Vernon and Elizabeth Hassett studied the latest statement of the balance in their joint bank account and scribbled sums on the backs of old envelopes. Dr. Milton played squash with the vicar and got beaten, as usual.

At 10:00 P.M. Spence and Laurel met at the location they had arranged earlier, on the northern perimeter of the grounds of Marlby Manor. After checking over their plans in some detail, they went their separate ways again.

Susan Green was at home, playing Scrabble with Detective Sergeant Wilberforce. Home in her case was a small cottage situated at the north gate of Marlby Manor. Outside, one large policeman was located up an old oak tree, armed with a two-way radio set, and hidden behind various hedges and bushes were four other officers, all in radio communication with each other. The cars that had brought them here were parked well back among the trees on the estate, totally out of sight.

"Twenty-five points to me, I think," said Susan as she placed her final letter on the Scrabble board.

Wilberforce coughed. "Um — not quite, Miss Green," he said politely. "I think you'll find that acquire has a 'c' in it."

Susan looked down at the board. "Oh dear," she said nervously. "I'm so sorry. You're right, of course; I don't usually make mistakes like that. It's just that I'm so very much on edge tonight — I can't seem to concentrate."

Wilberforce smiled comfortingly. "Don't worry, Miss. It'll soon be over."

Susan gnawed on her thumbnail anxiously. "I do hope so," she said earnestly. "I really do." Her voice was tight and tense, and she jumped with fright as there was a sudden click at the window. "What's that?" she squawked.

Wilberforce glanced casually toward the source of the sound. "Nothing much," he said. "Just a branch of the rosebush tapping against the glass. At least ... I think that's what it was."

*

In the summerhouse, beside the lake on the grounds of Marlby Manor, Detective inspector Laurel looked at his watch for the umpteenth time. He had bought a new watch only recently, a digital model with a little light that came on when he pressed a button. Very useful on assignments like this, but it didn't make the time pass any quicker, particularly when he was cramped and uncomfortable and waiting for a murderer. His watch told him that it was still only half past ten, and the murderer's invitation had been for eleven o'clock. He gave a silent sigh and tried hard to relax.

Laurel had quite a good view from his hiding place, though he himself was made almost completely invisible both by the back of an old wicker chair and by the dark shadows within the summerhouse. Moonlight provided some degree of illumination, and his eyes were now well adjusted to the gloom. Through the open door he could see out toward the lake, and through two small windows he could see open ground to the southwest, toward the manor, and to the northeast, toward the footbridge over the stream.

Suddenly, to his left, Laurel caught sight of a movement through the window. He looked again, wondering if he could have been mistaken.

Nothing. So he had been wrong after all.

But then — there it was again.

This time there was no doubt at all in Laurel's mind. Someone was approaching from the direction of Marlby Manor. A man, by the look of it, or at any rate someone wearing slacks or jeans.

Laurel shrank back into his hiding place. The three other police officers who were positioned around the summerhouse did the same.

And for some time nothing happened.

Then there was movement again, much closer this time. Whoever was coming had paused behind a tree. Waiting. Watching. Wondering.

The figure advanced, his feet making no sound on the thick summer grass. Then the door of the summerhouse was reached.

A dark shape filled the doorway, reducing by a fraction the dim light of the moon.

The man came in. He paused at the door, looked around, and then advanced toward the chair behind which Laurel was hidden.

He sat down.

For a moment nothing happened. Then Laurel drew a deep breath, reached forward, and grabbed both arms of the man sitting in the chair in front of him, and blew loudly on the whistle clenched between his teeth.

For a few seconds there was complete pandemonium. The man in the chair shouted and struggled, twisted and squirmed, kicked and cursed. But it was no use. Three burly policemen hurtled in from outside, grabbed him, handcuffed him, banged him up against a wall, and shone a torch in his face.

The beam shone upwards, distorting the captured man's features, and he squinted and twisted up his face against the light, making it harder than ever to see who it was. It was a moment or two before Laurel recognised him.

"Well," he said, when at last he had solved the puzzle, "good evening, Mr. Bannerman. And what are you doing here?"

*

In Susan Green's Cottage, the telephone rang. Susan answered it.

"Oh hello, Lady Dinnister!" she said brightly. Then she listened for some moments. And as the seconds passed, the blood drained out of her cheeks, and her eyes opened wide.

Wilberforce looked up at her with concern. "What's the matter?" he asked.

Susan covered the mouthpiece with her hand. "It's Lady Dinnister," she told him. "From the manor. She says something dreadful's happened in the summerhouse. She says I ought to go over there at once."

Wilberforce rose to his feet. "Let me speak to her," he said.

*

In the road outside Susan's cottage, the policeman up the oak tree saw a solitary pedestrian illuminated for a moment in the headlights of a passing car. He used the noise of the car to cover the sound of one word spoken into his radio. After that there was silence. All the watchers were alert.

The pedestrian approached slowly but steadily. He turned in at the north entrance to the manor grounds and approached the front gate of the cottage.

There were no lights on in the front rooms of the house, and before opening the gate the pedestrian walked on a few feet and peered over the hedge at the side windows. Then, satisfied that there was a light on behind the curtains drawn across the window of the living room, he returned to the gate, opened and closed it silently, and advanced on the front door.

The visitor reached into his pocket and took out a key.

There was a long pause.

Then the man inserted the key, very quietly, into the lock. He opened the door, went inside, and closed it behind him, all without the slightest sound being heard by those who were watching.

Inside the house Spence was waiting. With a click, he turned on the light in the hall.

The full force of a one-thousand-watt bulb, which Spence had inserted into the light-socket earlier that evening, blazed out and bounced off the white walls, dazzling and blinding the man who had previously been moving in darkness.

The man cried out in shock and fear. He dropped the key and held up his hands in front of his face, cowering back into the corner where the wall and the door came together.

Spence stepped quickly toward him, a police truncheon raised high and ready.

"No! No! Don't hit me!" cried the man. He held up his hands imploringly, bending even lower at the knee to indicate submission. He began to sob and to repeat, "Please, please, don't hit me!" over and over again.

Spence, who had been prepared to hit the man very hard indeed if necessary, lowered his truncheon. He reached forward and lifted the terrified man into a more upright position. Tears were beginning to cascade down the man's cheeks.

"It's all right," said Spence. "It's all right, Mr. Tanner. We aren't going to hurt you."

Twenty-Nine

"Well," said Julia, after she had provided both her husband and Detective Inspector Laurel with very large drinks, "I think you'd better tell me all about it. You caught him in Susan Green's cottage, you say?"

"Yes," said Spence, taking a grateful gulp from his glass, "we did."

The time was 2:00 A.M., and Laurel had accepted an invitation to call in at Spence's house for a nightcap before driving on to his home.

"So it's all over bar the shouting?" Julia continued, pouring herself a more modest drink before coming to sit down with the two men.

"Yes, mercifully, that's right," said Spence. He put his feet up on a small stool and relaxed fully. "Mr. Tanner has been arrested and charged, and he's told us everything we wanted to know — several times over, in fact. Poor old Tanner — I think he was quite glad to be caught in the end."

"Poor old Tanner, nothing," said Laurel sourly. "He's a nasty, vicious criminal, and he deserves to be locked away for a very long time."

Spence chuckled. "Yes, well, that's true," he admitted. "But he certainly got a very bad shock when I switched on the light and jumped out at him. I could hardly get him to stop talking long enough to write down what he was saying. However, in the end we got what we wanted — a detailed statement, signed, sealed, and delivered, with the how, the why, and the wherefore."

"Oh," said Julia with interest. "And what were the how, the why, and the wherefore?"

Spence took another drink before answering. "Well, the means used to carry out the crime was much as we thought: arsenic in the form of weedkiller, taken from the gardener's shed. Old Tanner was quite a familiar figure in the local library, and once he'd decided to murder Miss Fosdyke, he read up about poisons in the hope of finding something close at hand which he wouldn't have to buy specially. He'd killed a number of enemy soldiers in his army days during the war, apparently, but violent physical assault in peacetime was not his style at all. And, in any case, he realised that a direct assault would leave far too many traces on his clothes, and so forth. He did think about poisoning Fosdyke over a long period of time, but that was too difficult to administer, and he thought the doctor would probably recognise the symptoms of poisoning if they persisted for more than a few days. So in the end he decided on using a single dose of arsenic, which in fact was a very smart move indeed."

"The results could easily have been mistaken for an attack of gastroenteritis," said Laurel. "Many doctors might have signed the death certificate without thinking twice about it."

"Well, yes," said Julia, "I can understand all that. But what was his motive?"

"Well," said Spence, "in a nutshell, Tanner thought that Miss Fosdyke was going to get him sacked. And he didn't want to be sacked, so he killed her."

"And *was* she going to get him sacked?"

Spence shrugged. "Who can say? We shall never know for certain exactly what she intended. But I'm pretty sure she had decided to get rid of him, yes. The point was, you see, Miss Fosdyke had had dealings with Tanner before, when she was a hospital almoner. Ten years ago Tanner was admitted to Wellbridge General with violent abdominal pains, and none of the doctors could decide what was causing them. In fact, they were probably caused by all his domestic problems because his life was pretty much a shambles at that time."

"In what way?"

"Well, he had been married, but he'd fallen out with his wife and daughter and had left home. He had kept a pub, but the brewery had kicked him out, and now he was unemployed."

"I see. Did they sack him because he drank too much?"

"No, strangely enough, they didn't. He did drink, but not to excess. No, gambling was Tanner's main vice, and he was a loser, of course, as they all are. He had very large debts, so he borrowed to pay them off, and then gambled all that money away, and so on — it's the usual story with inveterate gamblers. And so eventually, when he ended up in hospital, Fosdyke had to deal with large numbers of creditors who wanted to know when he was going to be able to pay them. They were a damn nuisance to her, and she decided, on the basis of her experience then, that Tanner was a spendthrift and a malingerer and a very fluent liar. He was devious and difficult and totally untrustworthy."

"He didn't have a criminal record, though, did he?" asked Julia.

"No," said Spence, "I'll give him that. Either he'd always stayed just within the bounds of the law, or else he'd been very lucky. In any event, the long and the short of it was that ten years ago Miss Fosdyke formed a very poor opinion of Tanner indeed. It's all on the file that she wrote at the time. The doctors could find nothing at all specifically wrong with him, and after a couple of weeks he was discharged from the hospital to solve his own problems as best he could."

"Hmm. And then what?"

"Then nothing, at least for the next ten years or so. Tanner drifted around for a bit, had one or two odd jobs in country houses, and eventually got taken on as Lady Dinnister's butler. From then on, as far as he was concerned, everything in the garden was rosy. He says himself that he'd realised by that stage that if he wasn't going to go under completely, he had to pull himself together a bit. Do a reasonable day's work and not bet more on the horses than he could afford. And for seven years or so, all went swimmingly."

"Until Miss Fosdyke appeared again?"

"Yes."

"And she remembered him, I suppose?"

"Oh yes. And he remembered her, of course. Though for a while neither of them let on. However, almost immediately after she arrived at Marlby Manor, Miss Fosdyke must have decided that she wasn't at all happy about having this man working and living under the same roof as herself, even if Lady Dinnister did find him a satisfactory butler. So before long she had a look at his employment file in Miss Green's office."

Julia smiled. "And found, I suppose, that when applying to Lady Dinnister for a job, he'd been less than frank about his previous life."

Spence nodded. "Yes, that's right. Not to put too fine a point on it, he'd forged his testimonials. Done it quite cleverly, too, I must say. He wrote a letter from an imaginary nobleman who was just going abroad on a cruise, saying what an excellent fellow Tanner was, and how sorry he was to lose him, and so forth. The nobleman explained that he would be abroad for some time, so Lady Dinnister just took the testimonial at face value and never bothered to check up on it."

"Oh dear."

"Yes. Oh dear. However, Miss Fosdyke soon spotted it for a forgery, so about two months ago she and Alfred Tanner had a little chat."

"What did she tell him? That he had to go, or she would blow the whistle on him?"

"Yes, that's about it. But apparently Miss Fosdyke had a very strong respect for the ethics of her former profession."

"Confidentiality, you mean."

"Yes. As far as she was concerned, what had passed between her and Tanner in the hospital ten years ago was very much a secret."

"So she didn't tell Lady Dinnister about it?"

"No. Nor had she told Lady Dinnister about the forged references. And after seven years' good service from Tanner, Lady Dinnister probably wouldn't have been too interested anyway. No, what Fosdyke did do was to tell Tanner that she didn't think he was a reliable enough person to stay on in his present post. He was still a gambler — that was well known — and he was also running one or two little fiddles that Fosdyke found out about."

"What, you mean milking the petty cash?"

"Yes, that sort of thing. What he was actually doing was getting kickbacks from a couple of the firms who were doing regular business with the manor. Nothing much, just the usual little perks that are very easy to arrange in a job like that, if you're so inclined. Hazel is as honest as they come, and Susan Green is too young and naive to spot any irregularities. But Fosdyke soon saw what was happening, and she gave Tanner an ultimatum. He had three months to find himself a job elsewhere, and if he didn't go, she would tell Lady Dinnister about his various little misdemeanors."

"Hmm," said Julia. "She must have been quite an old battle-axe."

"Oh, she was," said Spence. "She was. Of course Tanner got on pretty well with Lady Dinnister, but he knew that Fosdyke had a lot more influence with her than he did, and he had no doubt whatever that Fosdyke could get rid of him if she wanted to."

"And the three months were nearly up, I suppose?"

"Yes. Now look at it from Tanner's point of view, and you can see how desperate he really was. For seven years he'd lived in a warm, comfortable house, with good food, an undemanding job, and an employer who had a bet occasionally herself. What more could he possibly wish for? And where else could he possibly go? He's sixty-four years old; who wants a sixty-four-year-old butler? All he wanted to do now was to hang on where he was until Lady Dinnister died, when he could inherit enough to buy himself a little cottage somewhere and end his days in reasonable comfort and peace."

"And Miss Fosdyke was putting all that at risk."

"She was indeed. If Fosdyke got him sacked, he would lose his expected inheritance and everything else with it. He would have nowhere to go, and he wouldn't have a penny to his name. It's a remarkable thing, but that room of his is almost completely bare of personal possessions — because he's gambled it all away, of course. All he would have had when he reached the age of sixty-five would have been the old-age pension."

"And I wouldn't care to have to live on that," said Laurel.

"Nor me," echoed Spence.

"So he decided to poison her," said Julia sadly.

"Yes. Tanner was too old and too tired to start all over again. He wanted to stay where he was, and he felt the most intense bitterness and resentment of this busybody who was trying to drive him away. After a few days he had convinced himself that Fosdyke actually *deserved* to get poisoned. And, as I've said, he read up on it and worked out a plan. It wasn't difficult because, as the butler, he had keys to all the rooms, and as far as I can discover, Miss Fosdyke never locked her room anyway."

"But why did he leave that typewritten compliments slip?"

"Well, he'd heard Lady Dinnister talk about possible attempts on her own life, and although he didn't believe that story, it did give him an idea. He would try to make Fosdyke's death look natural, and if that failed, he would try to make it look as though someone had attempted to kill Lady Dinnister."

"And in fact, of course, he succeeded," said Laurel.

"Yes, for about twenty-four hours," said Spence.

"But those so-called attempts on Lady Dinnister's life were just accidents, weren't they?" asked Julia.

"Oh yes," Spence confirmed. "There was no evil influence behind them at all — just negligence, like the garage not putting the wheel back on her car properly."

"I see. So it was Monday night when Tanner poisoned Miss Fosdyke's sherry."

"Yes. It was common knowledge that she took a regular nightcap, so he thought if he did it late one evening, there wasn't much risk to anyone else. He did think about leaving a false suicide note, but decided against it because Fosdyke just wasn't the type to kill herself. So he settled for hoping that it would all be put down to natural causes but prepared himself for the alternative."

"With the compliments card."

"Yes. It was fairly simple, really. On Tuesday morning Miss Fosdyke was found dead. On Wednesday morning I rang the manor to say that we were coming round, so he knew then that we'd spotted something amiss. He popped upstairs, topped up the sherry bottle with water, as we discussed earlier, and left the compliments card beside the bottle, indicating that it had supposedly been intended for Lady Dinnister. And by doing that, he threw suspicion onto members of her immediate family. If by any chance foul play had not been suspected, he would have simply poured the sherry away."

"Yes. I see," said Julia. "And even once you knew that Miss Fosdyke was the intended victim, and not Lady Dinnister, the relations still had the strongest motives for trying to kill her."

"From certain points of view, yes," said Spence.

"Well, how did you know it was Mr. Tanner then? Was it through the hospital file?"

"No. I didn't see that until after I'd made my mind up. No, what really put me onto it was that Lady Dinnister said that Tanner and Miss Fosdyke did not see eye to eye and that Miss Fosdyke thought a younger man would do the job more efficiently. Even that was an understatement, of course, because the truth of the matter was that Lady Dinnister didn't really need a butler at all. He was an anachronism — a hangover from the era of country-house weekends, and he knew it."

"But plenty of the other suspects didn't see eye to eye with Miss Fosdyke either," Julia insisted. "The Hassetts, for instance. They hated her guts for opposing the sale of the manor. And Susan Green disliked her for poking her nose into her love affair."

"Yes," said Spence patiently, "but consider their situation when compared with Tanner's. The Hassetts are really quite well off. Oh, I know they owe money all over the place, but they can and will pay it off. If worse comes to worst, they can borrow from Lady Dinnister, or

Elizabeth can go out and get a job. And as far as Susan Green was concerned, one of Fosdyke's main objections to Alec marrying her was the fact that he was still at university, which time alone will take care of very nicely, because eventually he'll finish his course. And in any case, neither Alec Bannerman nor Susan Green needed to take any notice of what Miss Fosdyke thought about anything, as you yourself pointed out. But Alfred Tanner was in an entirely different situation. Here was Fosdyke giving him an ultimatum in private and going around in public saying that she thought a younger man would be much better value for the money. So his position was quite clear. The passing of time was not going to help him. All that would happen to him would be that the deadline would run out, he would get older still, his arthritic leg would get worse, and so on. The only prospect facing Tanner was of unemployment in some lonely bed-sitter, with nothing to do except make a pint of beer last all evening. You said yourself, Julia, that a murderer has to be desperate; he has to feel fully justified in what he is doing. Well, Tanner met those criteria in a way that none of the others did."

"All right," said Julia, "I accept that. But once you'd decided that he was the one, how did you get him to admit it?"

Spence grinned and sipped his drink. "Well, I hadn't got any proof, and I didn't think I was likely to get any, either. So I decided that the only way to finish off the case was to get Tanner to do something incriminating and catch him off guard. So I got Susan Green to write him a note. What it said was that she knew he had killed Miss Fosdyke, and she knew why, and if he wanted her to keep quiet about it, he would have to pay her. She wanted as much cash as he could lay hands on immediately, delivered to the summerhouse at 11:00 P.M., and she wanted fifty percent of his wages from then on. She typed it all out at my dictation, and we left it in Tanner's room earlier this evening — or yesterday evening, I should say, since it's now half past two in the morning."

"Then what?"

"Well, later on Tanner found the note and did some very hard thinking. If he'd been really bright, of course, he would have smelt a rat. But I'm afraid he's not very bright — if he were, he would have been a bookmaker all his life and not a gambler. He was also very worked up and on edge, as you can imagine any murderer is during the course of an investigation. So he didn't doubt that the letter was genuine, and he considered his options. He could run, which would have been fatal because it would have given away his guilt. He could have caved in and accepted the blackmail — but he really didn't want to do that because it would cost him too much. His third option was to silence the blackmailer and be free and clear once again — because the letter made it plain that so far Susan Green was the only other person, besides himself, who knew the truth."

"And he chose the latter course. He chose to try to kill her as well."

"Yes. He did a lot of thinking, and he decided, at that point, that he would kill Susan Green as quickly as possible, before she had time to change her mind and talk to a third party. But he was a bit worried about Alec Bannerman either being at Susan's cottage all evening or else coming along at the crucial time, so he decided to make sure that Alec was somewhere else. He sat down and typed out a note to Alec, in Susan's name, saying that she would be out all evening but asking him to meet her at the summerhouse at half past ten, to discuss something urgent. Then he borrowed Hazel's car and drove over to Hattley. He sneaked into the Bannermans' garden and saw through the window that Alec and his father were both at home. Then he popped the note through the letter box and left. That way he knew, or thought he knew, that Alec Bannerman at least would be safely out of the way at half past ten, while Susan herself would still be at home before setting out to meet him at the summerhouse at eleven."

"That note would have had one other important effect too," said Laurel. "If Tanner really had killed Susan Green, Alec Bannerman would have been hanging around on the grounds of Marlby Manor at the crucial time, all on his own, with no alibi whatever."

"How did Tanner intend to kill Susan?" asked Julia. "More poison?"

"Oh no, that would have taken too long. No, I don't think he'd got much further than a rough idea of strangling her. It's very easy to strangle a woman, you know; it can be over in thirty seconds, and there's no blood. But in any case, as he got nearer and nearer to the cottage, he got more and more apprehensive and shaky. As I said before, face-to-face physical contact wasn't for him. And in the end, when he found me waiting in the hall, he suffered an almost complete nervous and physical collapse. If it had really come to the crunch, I doubt if Tanner would have been able to go through with killing Susan at all."

"And what happened to young Alec?" asked Julia.

"I caught him," said Laurel cheerfully. "I was hiding in the summerhouse to see who, if anyone, turned up, and when he arrived, we just grabbed him and then took him along to Miss Green's cottage to sort things out. The last I saw of him, he had his arm around Susan's shoulders and was patting the back of her hand."

"I expect he's still there," said Spence, "though he's probably patting something else by now."

Laurel chuckled and drained his glass. He stood up. "Well, thank you both very much for the drink, but I really must be going."

"Yes," said Julia, glancing at the clock, "it's awfully late for your children to be left on their own."

"Oh, that's all right," said Laurel. For a moment he looked a little sheepish and disconcerted. "I — um — I had a word with your friend Patricia North, and she agreed to sit in for me until I got back."

"Oh, what a good idea," said Julia warmly. "But what about her little boy? Who's looking after him?"

"Oh, I gather her mother lives nearby," said Laurel. "She's only too glad of an excuse to come round and give him a bath, and so on."

"Oh, good," said Julia with a smile. "Well, that's all right then. I'm so pleased for you."

*

After Julia had seen Laurel to the door, Spence poured himself another drink and topped up Julia's glass as well. Then they sat down side by side on the settee.

"Well," said Julia with a sigh of relief, "thank goodness that case is solved."

"Hear, hear!" said Spence in hearty agreement.

"Does that mean we're going to be able to go on holiday on Saturday after all?"

"I don't see why not," said Spence. "As you say, it's all over bar the paperwork."

"Oh good." Julia smiled at him. "It looks as if we've both been successful then. You in your murder enquiry, and me in my matchmaking."

"Oh yes," said Spence. "You're right. David Laurel and Patricia North — they do seem to have hit it off, don't they?"

"Yes indeed," said Julia. She finished her drink and turned to face her husband. She smiled at him affectionately. "Coming to bed, Ben?" she asked.

Spence gave her a sideways look and then a frown. "Now it's no good smiling at me like that, Julia," he said sternly. "I'm much too tired for anything physical."

"Yes, of course you are, darling," said Julia soothingly. "And you've got a dreadful headache, too."

Spence chuckled. "Yes," he said. "Come to think of it, I have."

Printed in Great Britain
by Amazon